CHILDISH THINGS

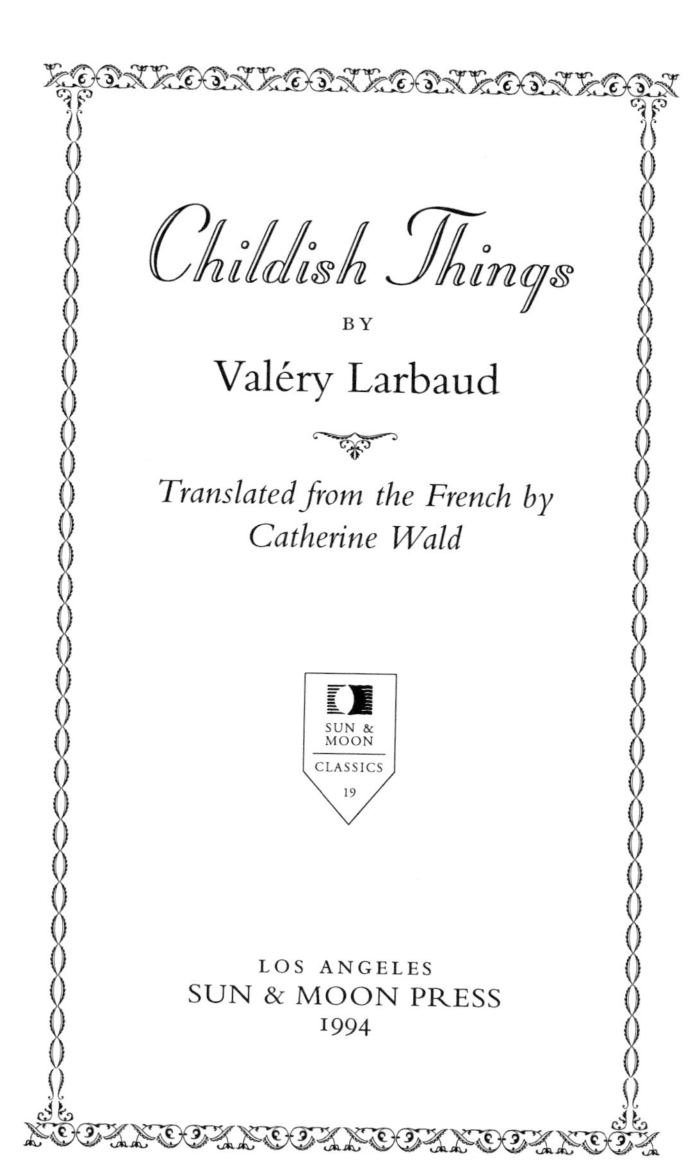

Childish Things

BY

Valéry Larbaud

Translated from the French by
Catherine Wald

SUN & MOON
CLASSICS
19

LOS ANGELES
SUN & MOON PRESS
1994

Sun & Moon Press
A Program of The Contemporary Arts Educational Project, Inc.
a nonprofit corporation
6026 Wilshire Boulevard, Los Angeles, California 90036

This edition first published in paperback in 1994 by Sun & Moon Press
10 9 8 7 6 5 4 3 2 1
FIRST ENGLISH LANGUAGE EDITION

Originally published as *Enfantines*
by Éditions Gallimard, Paris, France
Published by agreement with Éditions Gallimard

This book was made possible, in part, through an operational grant from the
Andrew W. Mellon Foundation and through contributions to
The Contemporary Arts Educational Project, Inc.,
a nonprofit corporation

The author wishes to thank Serge Gavronsky and Bill Zavatsky
for their editorial direction and assistance;
Debra Karl for her careful reading of the manuscript;
and Reb Cole for everything else.

Cover: Katie Messborn, from a photograph found by
Bill Zavatsky on the streets of New York City

LIBRARY OF CONGRESS CATALOGING IN PUBLICATION DATA
Larbaud, Valéry (1881–1957)
Childish Things
p. cm — (Sun & Moon Classics: 19)
ISBN: 1-55713-119-8
I. Title. II. Series.
811'.54—dc20

Printed in the United States of America on acid-free paper.

Contents

Rose Lourdin

To Léon-Paul Fargue

WITH OUR HAIR pulled flat against our heads by long, curved combs, and our pigtails folded up and encased in black hairnets, you can't imagine how hard our faces looked. And in fact, we were hard—on each other—and unhappy. At least I was unhappy in that provincial boarding school. It seems to me that in those days my feet and my fingertips were always cold; I was a sad and silent little girl. Whatever gaiety I have now didn't come until I fell in love for the first time. At my Jura boarding school, the schoolmistresses all said that I was "slow."

I had heard about Rosa Kessler before I saw her. It was my first evening at the school. She was certainly popular: the Intermediates spoke of her with loud shouts:

"Röschen...Röschen..."

I wondered how her name was spelled. Then I saw it written in chalk on a blackboard. I thought it was her family name: they never called us by our first names there. The older girls had asked me, "What's your name?" and laughed when I replied, "Rose."

I had to get used to answering when they said "Lourdin." It was as if, when we entered that place, we left our first names at home with our families. The only exception was Röschen, no doubt because "Röschen" suited her so well.

I used to love to be scolded. I think that I often did forbidden things on purpose, so that I would be scolded. Oh, it's not that this wasn't painful for me; quite the contrary. The first time it happened, I thought I would die. It was during the evening meal. The schoolmistress made a comment on my posture. I was very proud, and I thought I could lessen my embarrassment at being reprimanded by pretending to take it as a joke. I smiled, as if to say to the schoolmistress, "Yes, it's such a small thing, and it is really *too* good of you to bother with it."

That woman was nearsighted. Maybe that's why she couldn't understand the meaning of my smile. She suddenly lashed out at me, her face distorted, called me an insolent little thing, and screamed that she wouldn't put up with this kind of behavior. I was twelve years old then, and I felt that she was as angry with me as she would have been with someone her own age. The whole dining room had fallen silent. She sent me to stand in the corner, and I stayed there till the end of the meal, trembling from head to toe. All that night I cried, drinking my tears with my lower lip. When I stopped, I reflected on the schoolmistress' injustice. I squeezed this memory with all my might, and again the tears came. I ended up crying on purpose, thinking, "Tomorrow my poor eyes will make her feel sorry for me, and she'll repent. Then I will forgive her everything, and I will love her very much." I felt as if I loved her already. We would stroll together in the courtyard. She would become my best friend.... But she never did repent, and from then on I amused myself by making fun of her.

Another time I had accidentally written such a good dictation that the French teacher accused me of copying and refused to believe my denials. I savored my chagrin for a long time. I hugged it against myself; it kept me company for two days; and, when it evaporated, I was sorry to have been consoled so quickly. It was, however, an unforgettable injustice. Twenty years later I would run into that woman somewhere, and I would say to her, "Remember that dictation? Well, I didn't copy it." But those twenty years that would serve as my unimpeachable witnesses loomed above me, all black and horrible, like an enormous mountain range in a foreign country.

While I was suffering, I told myself that it was nothing, that this would pass just as my other troubles had passed, that at that very moment there were people who were much more unhappy than I, and, finally, that I would die some day. But I loved the taste of pent-up tears, which seem to fall directly from your eyes into your heart, behind the mask of the face. I hoarded them like a treasure, like a spring discovered by a weary traveler. So you can see why I like to be scolded.

But when I wanted to console myself right away, I had only to think of Röschen. She was thirteen in the year I'm talking about—one year older than I—and she was one grade ahead of me. She came from the German part of Switzerland, which was why she was nicknamed "The Prussian." I had not spoken to her yet, but I watched her as much as I could, and every night before

I fell asleep I thought of her tenderly.

During recess she always went about with the same two companions. She walked between them, arm in arm. I never lost sight of her, and soon I knew every feature of her lovely, fresh white face. She laughed a lot and had a certain bold way of throwing her head back and suddenly running off. The urgent and joyful sound of her feet striking the playground pavement became familiar to me. Oh, a storm was raging in my heart! I welcomed her presence with all my confused being, and I dared look at her only when she was far enough away from me. Her head and shoulders were large but graceful, her waist thin, her legs perfectly round, her skirt was already filled out, and if it hadn't been for her age, she could have been one of the big girls. Sometimes I managed to get behind her in line. Her neck was delicate, barely revealing the two tendons under her short, light-colored hair and her clear skin, which reminded me of the old tea roses of my early childhood.... I could not have explained how all this started: I loved her very life. Every drop of her blood was dear to me.

She noticed that I often watched her, and one day when we passed each other on the stairs, she turned suddenly and stared at me, her starry blue eyes, in which even the whites sparkled, full of malice.

And at one point I realized that I actually loved her more than I had loved my own mother and sisters. Evening was falling, the confident shadows stretched out between the stones of the stairways and the balconies of the old convent as if they were going to sleep there forever. I walked along a window-lined corridor warmed by the pink rays; and my heart was so heavy that I quickened my step, and, breathing through my mouth, I whispered, "I love you." From then on, there was a big secret in the world: mine. Other little girls, my classmates, had quickly surrounded me. I found them all boring or nasty, but I was forced to spend all my recesses in their company. There was one especially, with thick shoulders, a squared-off body with the face of an old woman, an unhealthy complexion the color of whey, cold round eyes that always had dirty circles around them, and the hoarse, high-pitched voice of an old woman. I can't describe the kind of disgust, even terror, that she aroused in me. Well, she was the one I tried to please, and to do so I humbled myself, always saying what I thought she would approve of, which was exactly the opposite of what I believed. The more odious she became to me, the more I flattered her, became her disciple, copied her gestures, anticipated her wishes. I got over this mania for self-abasement, but that creature and I were still considered two great friends. "Made for each other," they said about us.

As for Röschen, she had her two best friends and her relationship with the older girls. Everything separated me from her. And I loved to imagine catastrophes—like a fire in the boarding school—that would allow me to save her life, forever linking me to her in friendship. Or else I would have liked to tease her by passing her in the courtyard, making her angry, and forcing her to hit me. To be hit, or even shoved by her! But the very thought of her touch made me feel faint.

I didn't know much about her. I can honestly say that

I didn't know her at all, because I saw her only in the dining room, from a distance, and in the playground. I saw her, however, at close range at the end of that winter, in the infirmary during the evening study hour.

Toward eight o'clock Mademoiselle Spiess, one of the young schoolmistresses who was from the same country as Röschen, used to open the doors to the study rooms and stammer, "Infirmary!"

Then anyone with a cold or dressing to change got up and followed the schoolmistress to the infirmary in single file. Röschen used to take herb tea, and around that time I was told to do the same.

Almost every evening on the way back from the infirmary, when we were passing the door to the detention hall, Mademoiselle Spiess would shout:

"Kessler! Are you talking in line again? Go to detention, please, and wait there for me to.... What an undisciplined child!"

To be sent to detention was a punishment feared by all the little girls. I had never put myself in a position to be locked up there—to me, it was a disgrace, a permanent stain. Röschen went there of her own free will, smiling. I admired her impudence and her calm: it was almost heroic. And when she left the detention hall, her eyes were never red. I was so foolish that, had it been me, I would have never dared to show my face afterwards.

And yet, one evening, it seemed to me that she was purposely talking out loud and behaving badly on the way back from the infirmary. It seemed as if, out of sheer bravado, she was intentionally giving Mademoiselle Spiess a chance to lock her up in the detention hall.

One evening, when she left to go back to the dormitory, one of the older girls grabbed her by the waist and said a few words to her in a low voice. Röschen made a face at the girl, and the two of them looked at each other and burst out laughing. At that moment I felt a sharp pain, and struggled not to cry out. There was a malevolent look on that older girl's face. Röschen leaned on her, blushing, her lips half open, her eyes bathed in sparkling water. I couldn't sleep.

I had not yet spoken to her. I thought she was proud, rather insolent and stubborn, and a little "crude" as we would have said. And the thought that she had probably guessed my secret was unbearable to me.

Around that time the affection I felt for her took some forms that would probably look ridiculous to grownups. I was very proud to be named Rose, a little like her, and to make myself more like her, I started signing my homework papers "Rosa Lourdin." This made my schoolmistress treat me like a little fool. I was taken with her name, I thought it was just perfect for her, she was a big, blond girl who was always laughing....

Another time I took advantage of the long three o'clock recess to go upstairs to Rosa Kessler's dormitory, and I put on her extra smock. (During the week we wore black smocks that buttoned in the back and covered up all our clothes.) It was a great adventure; I remember every detail. I can still picture the three tall windows: strict white ladies, watching over the desert of beds. The subdued sky of the little town poured in through their empty eyes and spread out in bluish pools on the waxed floor. How my heart was pounding once I had closed the door behind me! I quickly slipped into the closet. As soon as I got there, I was safe. I took off my smock and took hers. This was the first time I put on a disguise: I had no idea that this would become my profession one day. Suddenly I heard a noise in the dormitory. I left the closet to face the danger. It was nothing. I hadn't closed the latch all the way and the door had opened. I threw myself against it and leaned on it with the full weight of my body. In a flash I envisioned one of the others finding out my secret, and the thought of murder crossed my mind. I went back to the closet.... Oh, this little student's encounter with a black smock! And I promised myself I would tell you the whole story without once hiding my face in my hands!

I pressed the cloth against me; I bathed myself in it; and I tasted it with my whole face. I also took the narrow leather belt. Röschen had written her name on the white skin on the inside. I kissed it lightly two or three times. I was going to buckle it around my waist when, suddenly, I saw myself as others might see me. It all seemed so silly that I quickly grabbed my apron, put Röschen's smock and belt back on their hook, and ran down the stairs all the way to the playground. Rosa Kessler was strolling there arm in arm with one of the big girls. I met her distant glance and felt reassured, and happy. I even dared to look her in the eye as I passed by, and I almost smiled at her.

One evening, on the first day back at school after vacation, I was very sad, and Mademoiselle Spiess met me in a corridor just as I was about to burst into tears. She was good to me. She felt sorry for me, and said:

"Lourdin, I have to go up to my room. You watch my office."

(She had a small supervisor's office in between the two study halls.) I said:

"Yes, Mademoiselle."

"Good. Sit down over there. Say, in case you get bored, would you like me to send for one of your classmates to keep you company?"

"Oh, yes, Mademoiselle!"

"Who?"

I was going to reply, "Kessler." But something in her eyes stopped me. It seemed as if she were reading my mind and waiting for my answer so she could burst out laughing. So I picked a slow student in my class who was stupid and boisterous and who teased me sometimes....

There were months when my life was preoccupied with the thought of seeing Röschen and the hope of rendering her a great service if the opportunity arose. But I was too shy to make any advances.

It was when I didn't see her that I felt closest to her. Did I mention that she was a good student? Yes, that year she won all the prizes in her grade. For that reason alone I would have liked to have been a good student. But it was impossible for me to knuckle under to regular work. I admired her for being a beautiful, carefree child and a serious student at the same time. What kind of future awaited her? She would be a famous scholar and a great artist; her beauty and genius would dazzle the world; while I, hidden away in the background, I would be her closest friend, her confidant, the sharer of all her thoughts. But for a start I was proud just to love her.

During summer vacation I found a nursemaid from Baden at the home of some friends of my parents. I went out of my way to find her. I wanted to ask her how to say certain things in German. My parents were surprised and annoyed to see me seeking this girl out. One day she finally taught me that, in the south of Germany, "Rosele" was the favorite nickname for Rosa.

And shortly after returning to school, I had this experience.

One evening, as Rosa Kessler was walking in front of me in a corridor where we were alone, I murmured:

"Rosele, mein Rosele.... "

She spun around, and turned on me with a worried look, glaring cold:

"How do you know that?"

She grabbed my arm. I answered in a voice that my emotion made ridiculously thick:

"Oh! I know lots of things."

"Like that?"

She stared at me fixedly. I felt she was almost angry. As for me, I was drunk with her presence. The moment had come to tell her that she had nothing to fear from me; that my greatest wish, my only wish in the world, was to be her friend. But I didn't dare: it seemed too much like a declaration of love! I was hoping that at least she would read the tenderness in my eyes. I offered them to her. And then I was sure that she knew. Maybe she would find the courage to say: "Yes." I would have needed no more than that. For one long minute we looked at each other intently without saying anything. She was the first to lower her eyes, embarrassed. I had let the moment pass. She let go of my arm, gave me a sort of friendly shove, and left, saying clumsily:

"Stupid kid!"

As for me, in that final moment I felt that Rosa Kessler was nothing but sweetness, tenderness, and obedience. I felt that if I could have called her firmly, she would have come back, and I could have made her get down on her knees, just for fun. And I felt that she needed my friendship. Yes, she was bigger than I, but she still needed my protection. There was too much sweetness in her; she was like a beautiful flower that any passerby could bruise. She ran a risk, I didn't know from whom; I was so far away from her! But it was an imminent danger, something ugly and terrible. I did not find the courage to call her back. And precious days passed.

Looking at her, fresh and white, with a whiteness that seemed to come from within her and flow across her face like the emanation of her purity, I thought, "I love you! And you are a good student. Soon we will be friends." The others didn't suspect anything; I had used so much deception and hypocrisy to conceal myself from them. But we will be friends, and we will force ourselves to behave, and we will lovingly obey our teachers, and you will always be pure and happy, because I love you!

Yes, I would dare to tell her all that soon, as soon as class was dismissed. I succeeded in running toward her, and suddenly I stopped, out of breath, my heart beating irregularly, my head lost. I put off my plan until later.

The right moment never came. Oh! The nights that I spent, sobbing and calling Röschen in a soft voice!

That year, a little before Christmas, Mademoiselle Spiess left the boarding school. The rumor went around that she had been sent away for making improper remarks in front of the little girls. But no one knew exactly which little girls were involved. Around that time, one of the big girls made me her scapegoat. She made me stand up in the snow in the corner of the courtyard, or else she made me hop on one foot from one end of the courtyard to the other. I was defenseless against her. Even now I have no defenses against affronts and mockery: life hasn't taught me anything. I can't even say that I hated that girl: I put up with her, waiting for her to wear herself out. My only revenge was to think that I suffered much more from the disgust that she inspired in me than from her meanness. But because I was ashamed to be treated like that in front of Röschen, I pretended I believed that it was a game that the big girl and I had made up. She was so stupid that she thought I didn't understand. She redoubled her meanness, and I was completely miserable.

When we came back from New Year's vacation, Rosa Kessler was nowhere to be found. I understood that she was not coming back. One of the teachers told us that her family had withdrawn her from school. I remember the sky that day: all white light. It was as if there were a white sheet of paper glued to each window. However, evening came. I felt even more alone than I felt on my first evening back at school after my first vacation. Rosa Kessler would never come back. I accepted this blow the way one accepts death, and I went, of my own accord, with a horrid pleasure, to find that big girl who tortured me, and put myself at the mercy of her whims. She made me embrace the cast-iron columns in the courtyard....

Months passed, with the routine of weekdays and Sundays. And one evening when only a few of us had come back from vacation and were all alone in the study hall, someone mentioned Rosa Kessler. I immediately pretended to be distracted, and I was much too upset to listen to anything.

They were already talking about something else when the girl who sat next to me in class, that dwarf with the old woman's face, came up to me and said in a soft voice:

"The Prussian is missed here. At least by one person."

I found the strength to ask:

"Who?"

But the blow had already struck home.

"By you, Lourdin, my girl."

I didn't say anything. I could have killed her. She went on:

"Oh, come on, don't feel bad about it! You don't know. It seems that it's because of her that Mademoiselle Spiess was sent away. Yes, they say that they locked themselves up in the detention hall, and that Mademoiselle Spiess showed her pictures—horrors, my dear, horrors! And they also say that the two of them smoked like men. Almost all the big girls knew about it; one of them must have snitched on her and that's why they threw your darling out...."

I never heard anyone speak of Röschen again. One day, the year I performed at the Grand Theater of Geneva, I passed through the town where our boarding school was, and I went to see the photographer who took pictures of the group of students every year. He had saved the old plates, and I was able to pull out the group we were in, Rosa Kessler and I.

When he gave me the print, what a surprise! All those little girls in uniforms, with Chinese hairstyles—was that really us? What poor orphans we looked, what sad little faces! And rough and uncultivated, like boys' faces.

On the steps I recognized looks and postures forgotten for nearly fifteen years. Suddenly names from the past came out of the depths of my memory, with a confused jumble of facts that made me recognize already formed personalities. The big girl who made me suffer, for example: plump cheeks, high and flat, where her long face boxes in small, deep-set eyes, insolent and self assured, eyes that know that the world won't change while they slowly bat their thick eyelashes. You see, she was due to become a rich heiress one day. Me, I'm there on her left. Someone said to me: "How well-behaved and sad you look!" Really, how could anyone believe that this obedient little girl was so madly in love?

The teachers encircled the group. I recognized Mademoiselle Spiess. How pretty she looked, standing tall and thin, with her big white false collar and her fluffy, light-colored hair. She had a habit of blowing in the air to remove an undisciplined strand of hair that kept falling back down over her eyebrow. She had seemed very ugly to me when I was young. And me, with my big chestnut-brown eyes and my long eyelashes, I was much prettier than I had thought. Mademoiselle Spiess must be forty years old now.

Röschen is sitting next to her in this group, in the first row. Almost immediately she came back to me in a flash, and with her my former wild love, all my wasted affection and jealous rage. "Mein Rosele," the great passion of my twelfth year. I just smiled out of sheer cowardice.

Still, very often, when I am alone, I suddenly see the world all lit up, the way a glance from her once made it. I am twelve and she is thirteen. We have finally become friends. Two little girls hold each other by the waist, intertwining their arms and hands. I rediscover her this way in the depths of all my joys (I turn to her only when my face is happy); and all goodness, and all music: that's her. Then, just as quickly, my present life catches up with me. I come back and on the table I find newspaper clippings that are all about me.

There. But I didn't tell you any of the important things. Oh! The color, the sound, the face of those old childhood days without history. The solitary voice of our bell, at the end of a long sunrise filled with ever-increasing bird songs; the acacias blooming in the courtyard all night long in the depths of my sleep like a taste; the new smell of my uniform on Sunday mornings, when a long day without classes stretched before me, a day that I could spend thinking of her....

How this street at the edge of the empty restaurant wounds my eyes, like a checkerboard with its whiteness cut up by harsh shadows! Look—I ate breakfast at that table in the corner, on the left, the day I left for my

Brazilian tour some years ago. What has changed? Ah, yes: I became famous! Surely, if she is still alive, she has heard of me. But only with my stage name; and she doesn't know that it's the little Lourdin. Then again, she may have forgotten me: after all, we hardly knew each other.

The Butcher Knife

To André Gide

AT ABOUT two o'clock in the afternoon, the men go down to smoke in the garden in front of the house. They are distinguished men, gentlemen from Paris; among them are a prefect and a senator. Sitting on the green benches, their legs crossed, they savor their cigars and grow fat in the thick silence in the country, ten miles from any village.

Beneath the August sky, the fields stretch out to the edge of the garden. First they stretch out, and then they climb the hill opposite. This is as far as you can see in that direction. On the crest of the hill is a farm, a long white building with a brown roof. With the white sky as a background, it looks as tiny as a drawing in a book.

"That farm is outside my property," says Monsieur Raby to his guests. He is modest. After all, one can't own everything.

Devincet, the farmer, laughs huskily. Then he speaks, while repeatedly rubbing his fat hand across his mouth, a gesture which lends weight to his words.

"That farm? You'll have it whenever you want it, Monsieur Raby. With the life he leads—Moulins and gambling in the winter, Riveclaire and, with your permission, sir, women in the summer—Grenet Junior will soon have eaten it all away. Take your time, Monsieur Raby. You can have the whole thing for a song in a couple of years."

"It seems that it's already mortgaged to the hilt," murmurs Monsieur Raby.

Emile Raby, "Milou," who will be eight years old on the 29th of this month of August, and who counts the days as if this date will bring a tremendous change in his life, interrupts Devincet:

"Say! I'll buy that farm with my savings next week: I'll be old enough."

He is upset because no one is paying attention to him, and Devincet's voice makes him angry. He hates this fat man with his ruddy cheeks. He tries to think of a good insult. He can't find one, and he feels like he's being crushed both by Devincet's heaviness and by the solemnity of the words that are spoken around him. These matters of interest that he can't understand, and that are above.... Ah! Just when he has totally given up, look what he comes up with:

"When *I'm* grown up, I'm going to be just like Grenet Junior. I'll eat everything, and die dirt poor!"

Nuts! Devincet bursts into his phony laughter; he finds Monsieur Emile hilarious. But the arrow hasn't completely missed its mark: Monsieur Raby looks embarrassed. Milou is glad of it: he has succeeded in wounding his father. Anyway, why do he and his friends constantly talk about ugly, confusing things: chattel, usufruct, contract, conveyance? And the tone of voice the grown-ups use to pronounce these words from their special language! Milou would like to slap these gentlemen.... An usufruct is an apple that has fallen in the grass and rotted, all shriveled up and split open in the November rains. Conveyances are horrible black scaffoldings that are put in front of the white facades of houses.

Milou resolves never again to listen to what grown-ups say. He draws back a little on the bench where he's sitting, to make room for Dembat and Little Rose, who are not visible people, but who are much more worthy of interest than Devincet and all of Papa's friends.

It isn't enough to say that Dembat is Milou's intimate friend and his brother. He is Milou himself, but invisible and grown into a man. Free from reality and projected into the future, Dembat wanders through all the countries that you see on maps and in books by Lieutenant-Colonel Gallieni. (Milou doesn't like Jules Verne, because those things didn't really happen.) Dembat is a man of action: he's going out to see the world. He has a white helmet on his head; he advances across Fouta-Djallon; he visits the countryside of Peuls and Toucouleurs. He's already been seen four times following the Niger River to its source in a steam-launch, accompanied by a small escort of Senegalese soldiers and sharpshooters. The river's great humped back turns slowly between the distant shores covered with palm trees, rubber trees, and vines. And, lost in the beating of the sun on the water, the tiny craft, flying the French flag, goes forward into the unexplored solitudes.

Little Rose is a child (about Milou's age) who was stolen from her parents by an Arab for revenge. She had escaped from the Arab hut, but when she arrived at the French encampment, the sentinel fired and the little girl passed out, her arm broken. She is very blond and gentle. (She looks a tiny bit like a little Swedish girl that Milou saw at the Children's Ball last summer in Riveclaire.) Her broken arm still bothers her, but Milou and Dembat have taken her in and are protecting her, and now she has almost stopped being unhappy.

For a moment Milou and Dembat and Little Rose leave Africa and go for a walk in the woods that you can see from the lawn at Espinasse. It's a little spot in the Bourbonnais, the loveliest region in France. The row of wooded hills breaks, and the elevation where Fleuriel stands fills the space, and in the background you can see Fleuriel's steeple and its parish. And behind that stretches a large gentle blue countryside where the windows of Charroux sometimes sparkle in the setting sun. Milou and his invisible companions are transported to the edge of the woods, below Fleuriel. They sit down in the shade at the edge of the road you can see down there. The forest's freshness reaches them in a gust of wind. They breathe it in.... Then Milou suddenly comes back to the bench where his body has been sitting. Dembat and Little Rose disappear (back to Africa, probably). Milou realizes that he is bored, and goes back to the house in search of his grandmother, Madame Saurin.

II

HE FINDS HER sitting in the dining room near the window, in a spot where she can observe everything that is going on in the courtyard, in the kitchen, and around the outbuildings. She would probably be pleased to catch one of Madame Raby's servants making a mistake. Then she could say, "My dear, you just don't keep your people in line!"

She lives at Espinasse all year long, except during the two winter months when she goes to the Raby's house at Monluçon, where Monsieur Raby has his big agricultural implements factory. Her servants are countryfolk, while her son-in-law's are city servants; "...and there's no viler race," says Madame Saurin. Seated in her armchair, which she fills up nicely, she never lets the kitchen out of her sight.

Milou jumps on the arm of the chair and stretches out unceremoniously in his grandmother's lap. Of the whole family, she's the one he likes best. It's because there's more gaiety in this sixty-two-year-old woman than in Madame Raby, who is worn out by the cares of her household, by the domination her husband exercises over her, and by an incomprehensible and bothersome thing that she calls "duty." On the other hand, Grandma Saurin is, as they say, in her element; a real woman. She speaks loudly, affirms and settles, never hesitating. And her language is energetic, full of patois words that she uses deliberately.

Her judgments are definitive: "That girl had a child before she got married. She's a slut." The war has left its mark on her thinking: she calls the garbage that you find at the foot of walls "Prussians." On a walk with Milou she says, "Take care, you're about to step on a Prussian."

The child is instinctively drawn to this mind full of certitudes, this will that has never been tamed. Of course, she doesn't belong to his imaginary world. No person from the material world, from everyday life, has ever been elevated to Milou's invisible world, the life that he invents. They are two universes that are completely separate, and in spite of the affection that she shows her grandson, Madame Saurin will never have the honor of meeting the Invisibles. The very idea of pronouncing Dembat's name in front of his grandmother makes Milou dizzy.

Nevertheless, from Madame Saurin he derives pleasures that belong to his own world. For example, he has her sing songs whose words he doesn't listen to, but whose music accompanies the visions of his hidden world.

Madame Saurin knows a lot of songs: songs from her day, songs by Béranger, and the political tunes that Monsieur Saurin used to like. "My Celine's Modest Lover," "Hey, Hey, Little Lambs!," "All the Young Students Go to the Cottage," "Voltaire, God of Common Sense...," etc.

"Grandma, sing me a song! You know, the Jesuits?"
Madame Saurin starts singing in a steady voice, keeping her eye on the kitchen window. And on the mantelpiece, the busts of Rousseau and Voltaire listen:

One pope sent us away,
He died of colic,
The next one told us we could stay....

Oh, the beautiful, brave music, in which fantasies of knights with golden armor revolve, in a country where neither the Marquis of Mores nor the Marquis of Mizon have been, in one of those lands that the geographers designate with the words "Unknown Territory," which Milou pronounced "Home Territory!" The song ended too soon.

"All right, now, let me go and see what they're doing in the kitchen," says Madame Saurin. "You go find Julia. She's working in the hallway."

III

HE FINDS Julia Devincet in the drawing room. Sitting on the best sofa, she's darning his father's socks. Julia, the farmer's daughter, is a twelve-year-old kid, big for her age, a brunette with beautiful black eyes and fat red cheeks. After her mother died, her father sent her to live for three years with his relatives in the south of France. From this brief stay, Julia Devincet adopted a very slight Gascon accent and good manners, and she never uses a single Bourbonnais word, except when she wants to make fun of the locals, whom she despises. But she speaks politely and reasonably to everyone, like a little busybody. She never forgets to say hello, or to ask about your health. Every year during summer vacation she has seven or eight new fables to recite for Monsieur Raby.

Madame Saurin, who regards her as the most innocent and well-behaved little girl in the world, keeps her at Espinasse during the two months of vacation. She feeds her, clothes her, and gives her presents. In return Julia mends a little linen, spies on the servants for Madame Saurin, and keeps Monsieur Emile company while she looks after him. Right now she's supposed to be darning Madame Saurin's stockings.

"Ah! I missed you!.... Has Monsieur Emile heard the news? No? Well then—I'm tearing up your crest."

"What crest? You've made up something else to tease me with, you nasty Julia!"

"Poor Monsieur Emile, how unhappy he is! That nasty Julia is tearing up his crest. I'll tell you, then: there's a new shepherd girl at Espinasse. Her name is Justine, she is eleven years old, she's a bastard, her mother lived it up. And she is a sow: it's so bad that at Mass they take up two seats, and they still only fit halfway. Her mother is a servant at La Feline. That Justine is a paragon of misery. She has seen so much of it that it's really funny! Listen to this! She lived with an old man who beat her up and didn't give her enough to eat. She was always sick, but he made her work anyway. One time she got her arm tangled up in a runaway cow's halter: she was dragged through some thorn bushes and across the woods for twenty minutes. Another time she made a huge gash in her left hand while she was cutting some vine posts with a butcher knife. In other words, she's had so much misery, pain, and unhappiness that I can't even look at her without laughing. See, just thinking about it, I'm twisting up, I'm curling up, I'm going to laugh myself to death! Monsieur, do you want me to roll in front of you on the carpet?"

"No, I don't like it when you play dog."

"Oh, he's mad!"

Julia puts her work down on the table, raises her arms over her head, shouting, "Woof, woof! I'm howling!" Then she continues, excitedly:

"To get back to the bastard, Mademoiselle Justine of

the Butcher Knife, I have an idea to amuse you: why don't we try making her even more miserable? We can swipe her things, make Madame scold her, and feed her food to the cats!"

"Yeah, let's make her life unbearable."

Milou, who enjoys taunting his grandmother's little dogs, is thrilled at the idea of using a girl as a scapegoat.

"And you'll go first, Monsieur Emile; she won't dare complain about the master's son. Tomorrow we'll begin our torture. I'll tell you what you have to do. And now, come jump with me on the sofa while we're alone. Your grandmother just put new springs in. Come on!"

"You know very well that Grandma doesn't want us to jump on the sofa."

"I'll warn you if I hear her coming."

And she helps Milou climb up on the sofa where she's already standing. They start by putting all their weight on the springs, which first bend, and then stretch back out, pushing the children up. Soon, they are jumping up and down in rhythm, their arms held tightly against their bodies, straight and stiff like jumping jacks. They fly, they soar. Beneath them the entire piece of furniture groans and shudders. A spring is surely going to break. But Milou, who has lost his head, is indifferent to all that. He has left the world behind.

Suddenly Julia gets down and kneels in front of him on the carpet. He hasn't finished wondering why she's acting like that when the door opens. Madame Saurin stops in the doorway, frozen with indignation in the face of such transgression. Julia runs to her, sobbing.

"Madame, I've been telling Monsieur Emile to get

down from the sofa for half an hour now, and he won't listen to me. You see, I was down on my knees begging him."

"Liar! Liar! And she's only pretending to cry!" shouts Milou, still standing on the sofa.

"Now are you going to get down?" asks Madame Saurin. "Little good-for-nothing!"

"Oh, my good mistress, don't scold me," coos Julia in tears. She kisses Madame Saurin's hands.

It's nothing but an awkward moment. Grandma scolds a little bit; Milou kisses her with sincere regret. And she leaves as the soul of the sofa calms itself.

"Julia, my little darling, I'm putting you in charge of Monsieur Emile. The minute he misbehaves, let me know."

With his eyes, Milou picks out the exact spot on Julia's bare legs where he's going to give her a big kick: there in front, on the bone—that hurts a lot. But Julia comes up to him, her hands folded over her heart, her eyes swimming in tears.

"Oh! Monsieur Emile, don't beat me, don't give me any more of those kicks that make me die. If you touch me, I'll kill myself: See—I'll plunge this penknife into my heart. I can't stand being bullied. Anyway, what harm have I done you? I warned you when I heard Madame coming. It's not my fault if you didn't understand."

Milou would have cried, if he had the nerve to cry in front of a girl. The feeling of having suffered a great injustice overwhelmed him. And he was so big and powerful in the invisible world!

"Monsieur Emile, be good! I beg you on my knees to

forgive me. Do you forgive me? Yes. Oh, how happy I am; I'll never make you angry again. Good! Now I'm going to give you a piggyback ride. Climb up on my back. Put your arm around my neck. There, don't be afraid to hurt me. Squeeze hard! Now you can spur me on. I like to be bullied. But don't pull my hair! Piggyback, piggyback! You aren't heavy, really! I think that, in spite of all your papa's money, you are not long for this world, my poor little baby!"

IV

The hanging lamp has been lit in the master's dining room. But through the slits in the blinds a bluish light reveals that it's still daylight out in the garden and the fields. The uncovered soup dish steams in the middle of the table. Monsieur Raby says to the valet:

"Pierre, send in the new shepherd girl." The guests at Espinasse are going to have a little fun. The door opens:

"What a nice little child," says the senator. Through the steam rising from the soup dish, Milou can make out a blonde thing, with hair, cut short, that doesn't curl (you really have to look at her apron and her skirt to tell she's a girl).

Her eyes are blue, her nose is large and a little long, and her cheeks are freckled. She crosses her little red hands politely over her blue and white checked apron.

Milou looks at those hands, and he finds the deep scar left by the butcher knife. Besides that, everything about Justine, from the moment you set eyes on her, calls to mind her suffering and the hard life of little shepherd girls. She tries to hide her misery beneath a polite and gentle smile, but her misery shows anyway, and shines around her like a halo. And right away, even before she has said a word, Justine enters Milou's imaginary world, next to Dembat and Little Rose. Hasn't she suffered just like Little Rose? (And for her it really happened.) You are suffering and no one loves you, and everyone always speaks rudely to you. That's why I'm rushing to meet you, and take you by the hand, and lead you to the best place, near my throne, in the country where I am king.

Monsieur asks the girl where she's from, to show that he knows the Bourbonnais dialect.

Justine replies that she is from Ygrande. Madame Saurin stares at her with her sharp eyes:

"Do you have more appetite than devotion, my child?" she asks.

When the person we love best is being interrogated, it is as if we are being interrogated, and as if that person will answer for us. Justine's hesitant glance meets Milou's eyes. In them she sees what she must say to please Madame Saurin.

"I have more appetite than devotion, Madame."

Everybody laughs. They wave her away and are still laughing when she has left. Milou is proud, as if he had been a huge success.

And from then on, Justine is part of his life, his real life—the one he lives in the invisible world, where he is grand and triumphant.

At Espinasse, Milou doesn't sleep in the alcove, as he does at Montluçon, but in a little bed in his mother's own room.

Monsieur Raby sleeps in the room next door with the door open. At midnight, after three hours of insomnia,

Milou can't contain himself:

"Mommy?.... Mommy?...."

"What?"

"Mommy, I want to tell you something."

"All right, what is it?"

"I want to tell you a fable."

"A what?"

"A fable."

(Milou knows very well that what he is about to say is called a poem in the "Treasures of Poetry." But it's a word he has never said out loud; it seems bizarre and exaggerated, and too beautiful, and he's afraid his voice will tremble when he says it.)

"You want to tell a fable? About what?"

"A fable called 'The Misery of the Butcher Knife.'"

"And that's what you woke me up for? Don't be ridiculous. How can a butcher knife be unhappy? That's silly. Go back to sleep, that's a better idea."

Afraid, without knowing exactly why, that his mother will notice the connection between the butcher knife and the new shepherd girl, Milou lies quietly and gets ready to make up his "fable."

But the words, all the words in the French language, are there, lined up like an army blocking his way. He charges bravely against them, first attacking two or three familiar words in the front row. But even those repulse his attack. And surrounding him is the whole army of words, motionless, deep, high as walls. He attempts a last assault. Oh! To master only one hundred of the words and force them to say this very important thing that he has to say! A last effort stretches his mind, which swells as if it's going to burst—it's a desperately stiff muscle that hurts.... He suddenly succumbs and abandons the enterprise, overwhelmed, with a sort of nausea and the sensation of an immense void within him.

And then he finds the one word that in some inexplicable way contains everything that would have been included in the fable called "The Misery of the Butcher Knife," and with his head under the covers, his hand cupped over his mouth, he whispers inaudibly: "Justine...Justine..." and finally falls asleep.

V

THE EARTH, to the angels' welcome, has just leapt black and smoking into Morning; and Milou wakes up in the cool room.

Around him everything is clear, with slender blue shadows in the folds of the white curtains. But suddenly he feels uneasy: like when you go to bed in the evening feeling fine, but wake up in the morning feeling an itch deep in your throat and saying to yourself, "I'm going to catch a cold again and Mommy is going to get mad." The uneasiness isn't coming from his throat but from a sentence that resonates inside him: "Let's make her life unbearable!"

What can he do to prevent Julia from torturing Justine? What will he say when she asks him why he doesn't want to play this game anymore? He searches in vain for lies. But maybe at just the right moment, inspiration will come to him. It would be better, however, if the earth could swallow up Julia.

"God, God, make her die right away."

But he's afraid that his prayer has already been answered.

"I beg you, God, don't make Julia Devincet die!"

When he gets up, he calms down a little. But he has resolved that he will do anything to prevent Julia from torturing Justine. If need be, he'll kick Julia to death; and he kicks a leaf of the dressing table a few times.

VI

THE 29th of August has arrived without bringing anything extraordinary. Besides, Milou possesses the best thing that anyone in the world could wish for: the presence of his beloved. (He sees Justine twice a day, from a distance, when she goes out into the fields and when she comes back behind her cows.) His birthday is just a day like any other.

Everyone kissed him and asked him to behave himself. Once again his mother led him to Monsieur Saurin's portrait in the living room. Papa gave his approval:

"Yes, that's the superior man you should model yourself after."

"But he'll never be able to hold a candle to him," adds Madame Raby in a voice that would discourage the best intentions in the world.

Milou, shuddering, stares with intense hatred at the portrait of the patriarch of the family, who was a deputy and who knew Gambetta. Ever since his mother forced him, after a scene, to beg forgiveness on his knees before Grandfather's portrait, Milou considers the older Monsieur Saurin the most hateful of his enemies. Still, the late Monsieur Saurin looks like an honest and intelligent member of the middle class, a little awkward in his "riding coat," which was the fashion during the Second Empire. Milou keeps staring boldly at the portrait. One of its eyes, in the shadows, spies on him. For a long time he has wanted to rip those eyes open with Julia Devincet's penknife. But what if tears of blood were to flow out of the torn canvas? Next to the portrait is a framed engraving depicting a short, fat man: Gambetta.

"Emile," says Madame Raby, "You must promise your grandfather that you'll become a man like him: honest and respected. Now, repeat after me: Grandfather, I promise.... "

A little embarrassed, Monsieur Raby leaves the living room. Milou dutifully recites the formula of the promise. But he immediately adds:

"And what do I have to promise M'sieu Grand Feather-Head?"

Gambetta is a deity in the Saurin-Raby home, a household god who is worshipped devotedly. Milou has just been slapped in the face.

The blow didn't hurt, but what humiliation! His mother rarely uses this form of punishment. He wheels around, intending to kill her. But she's already left; the living room door is closed; and Milou is left alone to face the rigid stares of Messrs. Saurin and Gambetta. He doesn't cry, but he lowers his head, not daring to look at the two idols. The hatred he feels burning in his eyes would make grandfather and the orator step out of their frames.

In a whirlwind of thoughts he remembers that the orator, during the Siege of Paris, had left the city in a balloon and thus crossed the enemy lines. Milou pictures himself in the ranks of the enemy with a pointed helmet on his head (and he's proud of it!). He aims carefully at the balloon. He can see the orator in the gondola, in a top hat and a riding coat, haranguing the clouds. The shot goes off as suddenly as Mother's slap, and the balloon falls, destroyed.

"Down with the Republic! Long live the Prussians!"

The first shout came out shaky and muffled. But his mouth soon became accustomed to pronouncing the blasphemy. Emboldened, Milou shouts, "Down with the Republic! Long live the Prussians!' over and over, with all the strength of his shrill little voice. After three minutes a sore throat stops him, but he really hopes that all the Republicans in France have heard him. Then he looks scornfully, almost with pity, at Messrs. Saurin and Gambetta. He has just trampled everything sacred. These simpletons don't scare him!

He trembles. Julia Devincet has just walked into the living room. That's because Madame Raby told her:

"Go find him, and make sure he makes himself presentable for lunch."

Julia looks at Milou with her wide, tender, and deceitful eyes, and runs up to him:

"Monsieur Emile, you've been crying."

"Liar! I was laughing, not crying. I paid them back for making fun of me! Just listen.... "

In one breath he tells her his plans: when he is fifteen he'll run away from his parents, enlist in the Prussian army, and....

"More of your stupid ideas, Monsieur Emile!"

"I *am* going to do it. You'll see!"

Without saying a word she draws him over to the sofa where she is sitting. He plops down sulkily.

"I'm not worthy of Monsieur Emile. I am Monsieur Emile's little servant, the daughter of his father's farmer, a little peasant girl."

He looks at her, a little frightened by this new tone in her voice. She goes on very softly.

"Will Monsieur grant a kiss to his little servant?"

And as he moves toward her, she orders:

"On my neck. Do it quick. Ouch! I'll lift up my hair myself. You always pull it. Quick, in case anyone comes in."

Beneath the little ear, his lips touch the white skin. Underneath it, a delicate blue vein beats. It's soft. He kisses her only once, and he really would like to bite her: This Julia is so nasty!

"You will notice," she says, "that *I* never kiss *you*.... Would you like me to tell you a secret?"

"Oh! Another lie!"

"No, it's all true, I swear. Anyway, I don't know why I should tell you my secret?"

"Yes, tell me, I want you to, I order you to!"

"Yes, and then you'll go tell it to your mother. You are so stupid. As soon as your parents are nice to you, you tell them everything you know, even when they don't ask you to. And then you are surprised when they take advantage of what you've said to get you into trouble. As for me, it's easy: I never tell my father anything. And he's none the worse for it! Listen, this winter, for fun, I hid some silverware in a pile of oats in the loft. My father looked for it for days: he accused everyone. And do you think I was dying to tell him where it was? I'm not so dumb! Papa has a heavy hand. They gave up looking and, one fine day, I gave my father a thrill by finding his forks. That's the way I lie. If Monsieur Emile knew how to keep a secret...the things I would tell him sometimes!"

"What about the secret you have now?"

"Okay, listen, and don't cry any more: *I'm tearing up your crest*."

"Not that stupid thing again!"

"It makes more sense than you do."

"Oh! I wish I were strong enough to give you twenty thousand slaps."

"Shh! It's time for Monsieur's lunch. I'm going to eat in the kitchen; that's my place. If you are unfortunate enough to repeat the secret that I just told you, I'll say that you forced me to let you kiss me, and that I caught the bastard teaching you nasty words. Oh! I forgot that I mustn't touch Mademoiselle Justine!"

"Lunch time, you naughty boy," says Mother, opening the door. "And try not to embarrass me in front of our guests. You've gotten your ninth year off to a good start, you scamp!"

"Madame," Julia says shyly, "I have reasoned with Monsieur Emile. I've shown him how good his parents are to him; he is sorry; and he promised that he'll never misbehave again."

VII

THE GUESTS at Espinasse are sitting down to lunch and speaking with more animation than usual; it's a celebration, and everyone at the party has a tall glass of champagne next to his big glass.

From his seat Milou looks at the countryside, which can be seen through the two windows in the dining room: the fields between the thick hedges, the long hill, Fleuriel's steeple in between the two forests. The countryside lies peacefully in the sunlight; it isn't celebrating Milou's ninth birthday. Does it even know that today is the 29th of August?

"Have some champagne in honor of our heir," says Madame Saurin.

"May he only drink it in the bosom of his family," says the senator, smiling.

Milou has already forgotten the scene in the living room. He is very cheerful, and his childish bad habits are given free rein. He asks the guests questions and puts his elbows on the table.

"Your heir is pretty lively," says someone.

"And he is an heir who will inherit!" cries Madame Saurin with pride, the pride that rises in the breasts of the middle class when they're dining, when they think of their position, their revenue, their future. A breeze laden with all this happiness floats above the table with the scent of the roast chicken.

The senator questions Monsieur Raby about the resources in the area. Are there any enterprises one might want to get involved in? Then there is talk of mines, of model farms, of economical railroads. Monsieur Raby has just mentioned the city whose name no one can pronounce without smiling, just the way they speak, in the provinces, about a beautiful woman who is a little flirtatious.

"There's Riveclaire-les-Bains.... "

Riveclaire...this name recalls the child's memories of scenes in a park striped with shade and sunlight, where mazurkas are sung, and where ladies dressed in white lace pass by. Their faces beneath their veils are as beautiful as Paradise, and they hold bags and purses of gold in their white-gloved hands.

It's a city that doesn't bother to exist unless life is good; it wakes up in the spring, and spends a whole summer in the shade of the plane trees. You would think you were in another country. The people speak unknown languages, and in the evening, beneath illuminated terraces, Neapolitans sing "La Francesa."

In the evening, in splendid casinos, you can see women pass by with bare arms wrapped in ribbons, slender bodies covered with a pile of flowers, jewels, and satin. On the thresholds of these hotels and in the shadows of these parks you meet beings whose faces you wish you would never forget, and whom you would love unto death if they weren't inaccessible and didn't appear to be from another world. That pink ochre sand has received the slender imprint of the most beautiful feet in Andalusia. To those murmuring mazurkas at the children's ball danced big English girls whose knees were exposed by their too-short skirts, and little Slavic girls who have an accent exactly like the rolling noise that the stream near our house makes. And at the height of the season there were the three daughters of the President of the Bolivian Republic: very young, gentler than anything you have seen in a dream, as pretty as holy statues.

Milou remembers the big hotels where Beauty sleeps through the summer nights, surrounded by perfume. It's a triumphant and cruel Beauty, a rich Beauty whose sight dazzles and breaks your heart. Once you have seen her you never forget her; even her memory hurts. Milou comforts his soul with the thought of Justine.

He sits motionless in his chair, but his entire soul is near Justine, in Justine's hands. And before her eyes, eyes that have cried so often, he rejects the memory of the beautiful strangers in Riveclaire who smiled into their flower-filled hair. "Justine, I am taking you by the hand." He hardly dares to press the little suffering hand that the butcher knife mutilated. He takes Justine by the wrist, that's better, and the two of them travel together on foot across the beautiful highways of France. She is tired, and he carries her in his arms. She is hungry, and he goes to beg for her at some farmhouses. "I will never love you enough for all that you have endured; I would like to suffer everything that you have suffered; then I will be worthy of you."

All around Milou the grown-ups talk. They are concerned with his future. The meal drags on, and the smells of roast chicken and liqueurs exasperate the child. Monsieur Raby is speaking, and Milou allows his father's voice to enter his world.

"In his position my son will be able to aspire to anything. A solid education in law, and.... "

"Yes, indeed, politics can get you anywhere."

"He's sure to carry the district, in any case: they would never dare to blackball Saurin's grandson," says grandmother.

Milou watches the peace of the sunlit countryside through the two windows; it seems an austere and indifferent presence, from which he draws a bitter consolation. These gentlemen who are plotting out his future disgust the child. He would like to insult them, scandalize them, to list for them all the bad words he knows: pig, slut, broad....

"But certainly," says the senator, "certainly, in the position that Monsieur Raby will leave him, our young friend will easily be able to hold the seat of the first magistrate of the Republic."

"Oh! Minister at least, or governor of a colony," says Monsieur Raby.

"Come now, you shouldn't speak that way in front of the child. You'll give him a swollen head."

Milou smiles haughtily. Their Republic? He repudiated it this morning. And these good gentlemen, who all look more or less like Gambetta! He can't stand it anymore. He's going to make a scene.

"Yet you, Justine, you suffered all the injustices of your

masters in silence." Henceforth Milou imagines that his parents are really bosses who pay him and who make him unhappy. He will refuse all their kindnesses. He will never get angry again, as he did this morning, and whenever he hears them say something that makes him unhappy, he will store it inside himself so that he can suffer even more. "To suffer as much as you, for your love, Justine. Starting today," he thinks, "I'm preparing myself."

"We aren't asking him for his opinion," says the senator, laughing very loudly. "What would you like to be when you grow up, my young friend? General, or president of the Republic?"

"Or ambassador?"

"Or member of the French Academy?"

Says Milou, "I want to be a servant!"

VIII

HERE'S A MORNING in the second half of September. It's been at least a week since the guests left Espinasse. The sky is less high than in August, and in the evenings the sun's rays stretch out for a long time across the meadows before they fade away.

Milou got up this morning in the usual way. It's not any old morning for him, however. He has decided to do something extraordinary.

He takes his time. He must choose the moment when the servants are busy, some in the bedrooms, others in the stables, and when there is no one in the kitchen.

Then he moves quickly. The butcher knife is right there, leaning against a wooden shelf near the sink where Milou spreads his left hand with the fingers stretched out. Justine wounded herself on her ring finger. Milou aims well, holds the butcher knife in his right hand, and closes his eyes.

A heavy blow, and his trembling hand releases the butcher knife. Then he opens his eyes, and his blood rises to meet his glance. It's horrible: a huge slash, just like *hers*. But it doesn't hurt. The blood flows gently, in little spurts. Justine will learn of this. Maybe she'll think:

"Hey! The same thing that happened to me happened to the master's son, and on the same finger of the same hand."

But it would be better if she never knew anything about it. If she happened to guess....

There is already a rivulet of blood in the sink; it follows the curve and slides gently into the hole ringed with iron.... Wounds are usually washed. They must have washed hers, too. Milou, with his solitary right hand, takes a little enamelware bowl, puts it under the faucet, and fills it with water. He plunges his bloodied left hand into it, and the cold water bites the open wound.

In the water the blood rises like thick smoke being pushed down by a heavy wind. Soon the blood forms a blackish, oily deposit at the bottom of the bowl. There's too much of it. Milou puts fresh water in the bowl once, twice, and three times, every five minutes.

The blood continues to flow. Now Milou's right hand is soaked with it, and soon he notices that there is blood all over, on his face, on his white collar, on the light cloth of his jersey.... And this blood just doesn't stop flowing.

He tries to move his hand a little. It has swollen up in the fresh water. Hey, what's that? He raises his hand one more time and realizes that the nail of the wounded finger is hanging, half-detached from the bone.

Then he jumps off, horrified, and runs to the room where his mother is embroidering in the peace of lowered blinds. He goes in, all pale, a terrible sight, looking like a child whose throat has just been slit. As the last scene of a tragedy, it's a huge success! He barely has the strength to say, "Oh, Mommy, look what I did to my-self, playing with the butcher knife!"

The ceiling comes down, spinning, and Milou tumbles flat on the floor.

IX

THE LAST WEEK of vacation and the second week of October is here. You can feel autumn in the plateau of Espinasse. A cool wind flows unhindered across the meadows, across hedges and arbors, and along the forest floor. The sky is a fixed, hard blue. The realms of silence are expanding in the Bourbonnais.

One morning Milou rediscovers his last winter's clothes, the way you rediscover old faithful friends. He rubs the dark thick cloth and looks the coming winter in the face. His finger, in its dressing and black leather sling, is feeling much better. But he's almost sorry that he didn't cut his right hand, too, while he was at it; because when the time for lessons and homework comes around and the schoolmaster says, "And your dictation?" he can say, showing his bandage, "M'sieu, I can't write."

Monsieur and Madame Raby get ready to leave Espinasse, where Madame Saurin will stay for a few more weeks with her servants. The full suitcases have already been sent to Montluçon. For Milou it's as if they've already left. He's planning an exquisite life there among his toys, and in the company of Dembat, Little Rose, and the most gentle shepherdess, Justine.

Because it's of no consequence that Justine will stay and live at Espinasse until next year's summer vacation. Milou takes his love for her, and her memory, and her image with him into his invisible world. And it's even better than having her near him; she is inside him. He doesn't even try to get a glimpse of her any more....

And one morning it's time to leave. Before closing up the chests and closets, while the carriage is being prepared, the grownups say to the children:

"Go play outside."

And Milou and Julia Devincet go down a garden path to the woods. In silence, because the grownups' will is a destiny that separates the children; it is significant in itself and needs no commentary.

Finally Milou, to break the silence, affirms:

"My finger is getting better."

(He really couldn't care less.)

"Let me see," says Julia.

He takes off the sling and pulls back the bandage. There is a poor little crushed finger, without a nail, stuck against the collodion.

"Pooh! That's disgusting!.... Really, I never would have thought you capable of that, you little bourgeois sissy."

"Capable...of...what?" says an anguished Milou in a hoarse voice.

"Put that thing back.... Yes, you must really love that pock-marked girl!"

Milou stops, and staggers, dumbfounded. An impure beast has just violated the sanctity of the Invisibles.

"Oh, of all the crazy things, this takes the cake! But

I'm telling you, I thought you were too much of a sissy."

"Julia! Julia! Julia! Julia!"

Milou howls, to drown out the blasphemous voice. Then he begs and threatens.

"Shut up! If you keep talking, I'll do something horrible: I'll stab you in the eye, or I'll put my hand under your skirt! Shut up. Do you want me to pay you to shut up?"

But he's the one who shuts up, exhausted.

"That's right, calm down, Monsieur Emile.... And don't worry, I'm the only one who noticed, and you know that I never tell tales. Look. First of all there was the scene you made when your changed your mind, in one day, about torturing her; that got me to thinking. I knew that you had seen her, in the meantime, in the dining room. Good. Then there was the way you talked about her, pretending you had forgotten her name or that you didn't recognize her when she came back from the fields, after you had spent an hour at the window watching for her! Do you think I didn't see through that? And the butcher knife!"

"Julia! Julia!"

"Listen, don't start up again. You noticed, however, that ever since that *accident,* I was very nice to you, and I very kindly kept you company while you had a fever. I didn't say I was tearing up your crest a single time, even though I was dying to! And then there was last week. The cows got chapped udders from sleeping in the wet grass. Somebody told you about it, and I told you that now they would be mean and dangerous to milk. Then, Monsieur Emile, who gets heartburn from drinking raw milk, went to find Mother Moussette to ask her for some. And he made her milk all the cows an hour earlier than usual. And you drank a bowl of warm milk without even flinching! All that so that the *other one* wouldn't get kicked. It's obvious! Ah! You would never do that for me, and I have.... Oh!"

Abruptly, Julia starts crying.

"You're just pretending to cry, liar! You're trying to make me feel sorry. I don't care—look; I'm laughing."

"Oh!" and Julia cries with all her might.

"You're pretending! You're pretending! And if you keep it up, I'm going to punch you."

Julia goes up to Milou and leans on him, so he can really feel her whole body shaking with big deep sobs.

Milou, defiant, deeps quiet.

Then she says in one breath.

"And me?"

"What?"

"And me, don't you think I'll pine all year for the sight of my pretty little master?"

"Oh! cut it out, I know you couldn't care less," says Milou in a trembling voice. "At least will you promise not to hurt her? Not to tell her anything about...."

At that moment Monsieur Raby's voice reaches them:

"Milou! Milou! The carriage...is...ready."

And they run back up the pathway without saying anything to each other. Julia wipes her eyes with her apron.

They stop, out of breath, in front of the lawn. The carriage is there; and Madame Saurin, surrounded by her servants, oversees the departure. Justine isn't there;

she's in the fields. Monsieur Devincet hovers about clumsily.

"Well, everyone is waiting for you," says Monsieur Raby. "Good-bye, little Julia, there's a good girl. Come, children, kiss each other good-bye. Come on, Milou, do you have to look so disgusted when you kiss a little girl? It's easy to see that you've never been in love."

The Hour with the Face

To Francis Jourdain

THE FIRST warm evening set up camp in the garden and posted a sunbeam on guard at each window of the house. Picture the outline of two pink cheeks, frank blue eyes, a big sister, blonde, leaning against the light. But you mustn't look round toward the window. Don't move. Don't even wriggle your finger. The clock on the mantelpiece says five past five. Monsieur Marcatte is five minutes late—that's a good sign. If only he were going to miss the lesson again.... Or if he arrived halfway through, then there would only be a half-hour of sight singing left. Don't move—the slightest motion could tangle up the skein somewhere along the line. Keep on sitting in the armchair facing the fireplace. And stay still. Like the open piano and the closed book where young Mozart, on the cover, is tuning his violin....

Seven minutes past five. Oh, go faster, Time, go faster! Ten tiny thoughts will harness themselves to the big hand and try to pull it a little faster toward its little sister who is waiting for it down there between V and VI.... The head, with blue eyes, and its pink and blonde shadows, fades from the window, and the stern evening sky scatters in white puddles in the mirrors, windowpanes, and polished furniture. And a little boy, sitting in an armchair, waits for his sight singing teacher. (A chair creaks.)

He'll ring the doorbell. That will give you half a minute to get ready to receive him, to take leave of the thoughts, so sweet and warm, that you were entertaining.... Quarter after. An obtuse angle has become an acute angle, and now the big hand must be falling more quickly (did they take this into account when they made the clock? Did they add some kind of brake to make sure that the big hand descends as slowly as it climbs the dial on the other side of the VI?) He could arrive at any second—to be a quarter of an hour late is nothing; but twenty minutes is already more substantial—then the chances of having a free empty hour will increase. It's an hour of crossing, like the trip from Pornic to Noirmoutiers. Five o'clock is the coast, which has already disappeared; five-thirty will be the open sea, where a white sun dashes against the black glass floor that heaves and falls as the mind tries to pinpoint the instant when the halfway point is reached. It may be a free hour, but it's also an empty hour, without play. Don't budge—the slightest motion would capsize the canoe in which, on the ocean of time, a small boy is paddling with all his might between five and six o'clock.

Luckily, as an antidote to boredom, here is the Face. It's easy to find when you know. But the child is the only one who does. He alone has seen the Face in the veins of the marble mantelpiece: a long Face, serious and young, completely shaven, with deep eyes and a narrow forehead partly covered by a crown of leaves. Its little black mouth is half-open. A little more so than last time, it seems. If only the face could speak! With what an unimaginable tiny voice, a "voice of marble," no doubt. No, it keeps its silence. Face, we understand each other without words. I've kept your secret, enchanted prince. I haven't told anyone that there's a face in the veins of the mantelpiece, and I've distracted people from looking in your direction. (Luckily, grown-ups don't know how to see anything, anyway.)

Noble Face, when will your enchantment end? Tomorrow, or maybe next month, or in a year. It will happen at night, or course. Your time will be up, and you'll leave the mantelpiece, and the next day there will be nothing in your place but the deep green of the marble and its golden veins, a handwriting that men have not yet learned to read.

In the meantime, Face, come sit in my little canoe. Someone has rung the doorbell! Now the door will open and Monsieur Marcatte and his sight singing will come in with the stink of tobacco and his old hands and thick fingernails, bent and stained brown by cigarettes. All the little thoughts hide, and the Face dissolves back into the marble veins.... False alarm. It was the back door.

Face, come back. Let's go for a walk together in the woods. (Isn't it funny how you can picture the woods, as if you were really there, while you're really sitting in the armchair. You would like to pay attention to this, follow this train of thought. But the pathways through the forest are more fun to follow. This is how a little idea comes, like a bee, buzzing up to the door of its hive. When it sees that the door is shut, if flies off toward some flowers.) A tiny vessel made of thoughts sails off to a country called the woods, carrying, in a precious little thought-up coffer, the noble, crowned Face.

We land, we demand entry at the port of leaves, we thrust aside the first branches, we dive into the green darkness. We meet a solitary beam of light. We follow the pathway of a thousand secrets. We cross the road of underbrush where all we can see are leaves, and above the leaves, a blue road, like the pink road of the forest, which is a road in the sky. Nothing stirs in the still light—except the little aspen tree down there, trembling in broad daylight—or maybe it's trying to signal us? Again we plunge into the shade and under some branches where the dry earth, beneath the hot grass, faithfully saves the old wheel ruts, remnants of a time long ago when they used to chop down trees (in those days you could see the shape of a hillside). And suddenly we're beneath the pine trees, the Imperial Guard of the woods, immobile and lofty, with their standards and pennants of red and gold.

But here is the path that no one has ever dared to follow to its end. It meets, at its darkest curve, a nameless, almost forgotten brook, its brown water trickling slowly beneath a roof of interwoven branches that it sadly reflects. Further on we cross a pathway that might lead to the Road of the Blindworm, but it's choked with trailing creepers covered with red thorns. Further on we find ourselves suspended over a clearing inhabited by a horrible tribe of giant thistles. And then there's a meadow with a lake, its two shores filled with washerwomen soaking their laundry. And after that comes a towering grove where a big sad bird, who lives there all alone, flies off suddenly with the noise of a closet door opening! And right nearby is the place where, one day, we saw a little iron cage next to a wolf-trap and, peering through the bars, we saw a grey cat with the blue eyes of a child pacing back and forth. And suddenly we are at the edge of the woods, on the banks of a wide stream, and on the other shore, where the meadow and the sun begin, we recognize the curve of the hillside and, looking up, we see a corner of the housetop. The path descends and widens and descends again, while a last branch tries to hold us back, and, crossing the wooden foot-bridge, we find ourselves out of the Tree Kingdom.

Face, noble Face, while awaiting our time of deliverance, let's take another trip to the sunset continents: the sky above the garden is like the blue and golden map to another world....

Ten to six—saved! Monsieur Marcatte won't come. You can move now, step out of the canoe, salute the Face (who remains inside the marble, a little bit sad and hushed, with its half-open mouth) with an imperceptible wink, and silently dock the dream canoe in the port attained at last.... Now we are out of the shadows and out of danger. A swallow preens its feathers after the storm.

But in the depth of the marble, the Face is still waiting for its spell to be broken. It will still be waiting when we reach the age of twenty, and the children who come after us will discover it in turn.

Dolly

To Régis Gignoux

DOLLY JACKSON died in June, 190-, in her twelfth year. It's been two months, and we—Elsie and I—already speak of it as if it were something that happened a long time ago.

Little Dolly Jackson died in the apartment she inhabited "with her retinue" on the second floor of the Hotel Royale: four windows on the Promenade, and three looking out on the garden. Her retinue consisted of a valet, two sick-nurses, and her governess, Miss Lucas. Dolly's mother is a famous American actress; and she was on tour in Canada when Miss Lucas cabled her the sad news. She had expected it, because Dolly had been ill for a long time. She replied by telegram: the body must be sent to the United States. All the preparations for this sad homecoming were made at the cheerful English spa. Elsie showed me the doctor who had supervised the embalming. What a frightful thing that must have been! How could anyone bring himself to remove her brain, for example?

I was Mademoiselle Dorothy Jackson's French tutor. Every day at four o'clock in the afternoon I went to the Hotel Royale, and we discussed La Fontaine's fables until five o'clock. The little invalid lay stretched out in a chaise lounge, and Miss Lucas embroidered near a window. Dolly often said to me, "As soon as fall comes, we're going to France, and I must be able to make myself understood perfectly! We'd be gone already, since the treatments here are too strenuous for me, but the air of the Midlands is so pure! By the end of the summer I'll be back on my feet again, and in the fall we'll go live in a beautiful villa that mother has rented near Menton." It was obvious that she would never again leave the Hotel Royale alive; and the lessons I gave her were not terribly serious. First of all, it was important not to tire her; and besides, do you really need to know French to get into Heaven?

And Dolly was not always a diligent student. There were days when I interpreted a story all by myself, without a second of her attention, and I told myself that I wasn't earning the money that her mother, that lovely woman, paid me.

At other times, Dolly was in pain. A fit of coughing. Was it some sort of strange malady? "You would think I was consumptive, right? It was funny when I used to go out after an electric shower in my bath-chair, to hear people murmuring, 'Phthisic!' They thought I didn't hear them. Some people are so stupid! What's wrong with me is my nerves, and the cough comes from my stomach; all the doctors said so."

On some days, she was in a bad mood: "After all, France is a country that is in complete decline. You can take a trip around the world without knowing a word of French." She also used to say to me, "What do you do with the money you earn here?" She asked for my photograph, and I brought it to her. "Oh! You put on your good clothes to go to the photographer's studio. You don't wear them every day. You're afraid of wearing them out."

But deep down she was very good. The day after those days when she had misbehaved, she used to fuss over me. She used to think that she had wounded me deeply. She needed me to forgive her, and she read "The Goat and the Rosebush" so sweetly that I quickly said anything cheerful that I could think of, just to block the flow of tears that I heard rising in her voice.

It was during one of the moments when her illness allowed her to be good that she said to me: "Bring me your Elsie, then. You've been telling me about her for such a long time: I want to see her. Miss Lucas says it's all right."

Elsie is a big, straightforward girl of twelve. She has green eyes the color of oceans that look at you confidently and reasonably. A persistent curl of her black hair often slides over her right shoulder, and would like to hide one of her lovely eyes, but she pushes it back with a brusque motion. I met Elsie in the schoolyard last year. With my cane I dislodged a ball that she had thrown into the branch of a young elm and was hanging there, stuck. We chatted; I went to her parents' house. They are working people. Since then, we've met every day and we're good friends. It amuses me to hear her say, "I love you with all my heart." For a moment I feel like I'm seeing her soul in her words. It's like leaning over still waters and finding that they're even more transparent than you thought.

When I brought Elsie to the Hotel Royale, I thought: a friendship will doubtless be born between the little student and my Elsie; and Dolly Jackson's last weeks will be the less unhappy for it. I was greatly disappointed. The luxury of the Hotel Royale intimidated Elsie, who became withdrawn. The waiting had enervated Dolly.

—So you're Elsie. And are you feeling well?

—Yes, thank God. (A silence.)

DOLLY: Where do you go to play? In Jephson Gardens?

ELSIE: Yes, on the days when it's free. On the other days, I go to the schoolyard.

DOLLY: But it's only a penny to get into Jephson Gardens!

ELSIE: My word! As Mother says, a penny is two hapennies.

DOLLY: Oh! I understand.... What a vulgar joke! (Embarrassed silence.)

The carpet in the living room was furrowed with little rails, switches and signal disks; and near the mantelpiece stood a painted sheet iron garage, full of little locomotives. The doors were left open and the trains could travel throughout the apartment. "This is my railway system," explained Dolly. "I have eight steam locomotives. It burns the carpet, but we'll pay them for it.... This winter I'll have them set up in our garden, in Menton; I'll make them build real tunnels on the hills, and real bridges to cross the pond. I'll have at least fifty cars!"

She had talked too much, and she coughed. She ended the conversation herself: "Very well, I'll probably run into you the next time I go out, in a few days." Elsie remained cold, withdrawn. She said, "Good evening," and we departed.

The next day I found Dolly dressed up and wearing gloves, as if she were going out. With her hat on her head, she remained seated near the closed window. It was the first nice day in April and, outside, spring padded all the hills of England with a thick greenery. "Tomorrow, or the day after tomorrow, if it stays nice, I'll go out for a minute in the wheelchair. Today is only a dress rehearsal. How do you like me in this dress? I think I must be at least as pretty as Elsie?" I told her she looked charming, but I quickly turned away: she might have read in my eyes that she looked like a little old woman, withered and worn out.

The rains fell, and Dolly didn't leave the Hotel Royale. She was feeling worse, and during her lessons I read and spoke alone. One day she gave me a bag full of candy. "For Elsie." Do you want to see her?" "No, that would tire me. The next time I go out. Tell her I'm sorry for being stupid and nasty the other day."

It was nice out again, and the chestnut trees blossomed in Jephson Gardens. But Dolly had to stay in bed, and Miss Lucas politely showed me out when I went to see my little student. I never saw her again. Every day I sent for news of her. Two weeks passed. And on the morning of June 3rd, the porter of the hotel told me that it was a matter of hours. We spoke in a low voice: no one must know of the visitor that was expected at the Hotel Royale that day. I decided I wouldn't leave the Promenade, I would keep the windows of the second floor constantly in my sight. Lovely, warm hours passed. Carriages and automobiles stopped in front of expensive shops. I walked up the Promenade one more time, up to the church. When I walked back down, the shades in the four windows on the second floor were drawn. I walked into the hotel lobby. It was all over.

I went to sit in Jephson Gardens. We were well aware that when we said, "In November...next December...." we were talking about a time when Dorothy Jackson would no longer exist. She was so ill that life and death seemed to mingle in her. We were well aware that after a certain hour, we would speak of Dorothy Jackson the way people talk about dead people. And that hour had come, while Elsie was in school, and it was nice outside.

Just then Elsie comes to join me. We will be sad together. She smiles at me from a distance. She'd finally stopped wearing her winter clothes, and she is wearing a big sailor-shirt, brand new, and almost as pure as she is.

"You seem all upset?"

"Yes," I said, "Dolly is dead."

"Ah! Good Lord! Poor Dolly! She was twelve, just like me."

"Just think: to die in a hotel, surrounded by strangers, because after all, Miss Lucas...."

"Poor Dolly, she had no one to love her but you."

"Oh! I should have loved her more.... Her fever prevented her from being sweet and well-behaved sometimes. Do the rest of us have that excuse? She deserved to be loved simply because she was ugly and sick and no one in the world would have wanted to have her as a daughter. If she didn't want to see you again, it's because she was ashamed of her illness; do you understand, Elsie?"

In the shade of a kiosk a military band plays some

Scottish airs. "Listen," says Elsie. "It's the song you like so much: 'Bonnie Mary o'Glengary.'"

I am silent, astonished that I, too, can pay attention to something other than Dolly's death. And Elsie has to restrain herself from humming the words of the song.

She is already looking for an excuse to get away from my sadness. She has a crush on one of her schoolmates, and today they have made a date to meet near the river, where there are sloping lawns that you can lie on and roll all the way down, laughing.

She has found an excuse, and it's the first time she ever lied to me. So I tell her I am going home, and I won't be going out for the rest of the day. This way she can enjoy herself without worrying that I'll find her out.

I watch her as she leaves. In the path not far from the bench where I am sitting, a sparrow scratches about among the grains of sand. Three little girls suddenly appear, pushing a little carriage in which a baby is sleeping. "Be careful," says one of them. "We could run over the little bird." They stop and bend down, hesitantly. The bird flies away.

The Days of Glory

To Gaston Gallimard

Chapter 1: The Three Heroes

LAST CENTURY—to be more precise, last year—the three heroes Marcel, Arthur and Françoise performed great and valiant deeds. You could say that, thanks to their work, the past century was the age of railroads.

Each of them, at the beginning of that faraway epoch, had brought—from classroom or boarding school, or from some other place of suffering where people live hunched over and locked up under grown-ups' eyes—each one had brought something he had mastered. Arthur and Françoise each had a song. Arthur's went:

Dance Pickaninny
Dance Canada
Like that—whee!
Tra la la!

When Arthur sang that song, moving his eyes, joining his arms over his head and slapping the ground with his ankles, he truly became a Pickaninny: a completely black, totally naked man, in a Canadian village square made up of palm leaf huts. You could see that he was a real savage, like the monkeys that Marcel had seen at the Zoological Gardens, beneath the glass sky of the hothouse. At that moment, if you asked Arthur something, he couldn't speak French; he would give a few strange yelps. The song and the dance stopped, and the Pickaninny once more became Arthur, the shop steward's son.

Françoise's song was long, complicated, and sweet. Neither Marcel, nor even Arthur, Françoise's brother, understood the whole thing. There were words that she didn't pronounce clearly, others that she half-swallowed. She teased the two boys by refusing to repeat them, and she said to them,

"I understand them, that's enough. Anyway, I'm singing in Chinese. And *I'm* the one who made up my song."

Arthur said, "That's not true!"

But Marcel thought that Françoise was certainly smart enough to have made up a song. He liked the refrain:

Beneath the bamboos,
Beneath the bamboos,
Ooh, ooh....

"Pickaninny" talked about grand, noon-filled days in a country like a hothouse. But "The Bamboos" described in minute detail a region of warm nights where all happiness dwells; summer vacations that are always just beginning, when they seem so big, so long, and so new that you still don't know what you're going to do with them; fountains where you can get wet without ever catching cold; and evenings when no grown-up ever says, "Children, it's time for bed."

And Marcel had brought back the memory of a vision. It was in the Country of a Hundred Mountains, where big black cities are inhabited by big blond men: the Auvergne. While the train was going around a curve, he leaned out the door, despite his father and despite his mother: it was his chance to see all the cars in the train squeeze together and double up, so that the engineer and the caboose-man could wave to each other. And from over there, in the forest they were about to enter, came a great mass of smoke. He was going to shout, "Papa, they set the woods on fire!" when they turned another corner and he saw this: standing on the two-railed street, a locomotive had stopped. You could see its smokestack, the two front wheels, and the painted red stripe that indicated its high rank. That was what was filling the forest with grey smoke striped with heavy white flakes. It looked like it was resting, like a man who went out to smoke his pipe in an alley in the park. It was alone and, when they passed it, Marcel heard its calm breathing and, in one breath, took in the smell of coal and the scent of leaves refreshed by a shower. He thought, "It came from Clermont-Ferrand to take a stroll over here."

From then on he paid careful attention to locomotives. He first figured out that they were the daughters and inhabitants of the Hundred Mountains: they were black and smoking like the great cities they came from, and to which they always returned. True, they went to Paris, but only because the slope pulled them and the plain invited them. Always, and from everywhere, they returned to the Hundred Mountains and climbed back up their slopes—puffing, scolding, hurrying—and hailed their homeland in the distance with great, pure cries.

He watched them closely. He got to know some of their habits. He saw that they are not, as you might think, serious and bored grown-ups. They know how to play. One, after a great drum-roll, sets off hopping on one foot around a curve. Others run backwards, leading a farandole of cars across the plains. Two others, stuck together, slowly pull into the station. Their sense of importance makes them raise their shoulders so high that you can't see their necks any more, and they march in step, whistling and playing their cymbals, and the whole station respectfully welcomes the Geneva-Bordeaux Express. Marcel even saw two locomotives attached back to back that were, nevertheless, going in the same direction. Are these things allowed? And suddenly he remembers seeing, a long time ago, five years ago (he must have been three years old), from the terrace that looks out on the park and the train yard, a completely white train. It was so beautiful that he realized that he mustn't mention it to anyone. And since then he has seen other trains that were almost as beautiful, especially at the entrance to the Paris station: some made of long yellow cars with golden letters; others crimson and black, like the one, with its locomotive dressed up in tricolored flags, that belonged to the President of the Republic.

Chapter 2: Retrospective

THAT'S WHY, beginning with the first days of summer vacation in that distant era—last year—the iron chairs in the garden were dragged along pathways, quickly forming a complicated network of two parallel lines in the sand. The direct line between the greenhouse and the villa was the first to be exploited. Then it was extended to the cistern. A little later, a line going from the villa to the pond was inaugurated. Arthur was the locomotive; Françoise, in a chair with wheels on it, was the passengers; Marcel was the Head Engineer, and at the stations he changed into the Stationmaster. Three trains per day, including one express, was the minimum decided upon by the General Assembly of Company Administrators. One of the expresses derailed and Françoise, recovered with a skinned knee, said she didn't want to be the passengers anymore. The children did without them, and she was put in charge of serving as a shuttle between the six big clumps of trees in the garden in a small local network made especially for her.

But soon the spirit of enterprise extended its conquest

beyond the garden. The central walkway of the park was crossed by a tunnel (imaginary) and a huge double track was established between the village—via the pond—and the billiard room. It was then extended up to the stable, which became the most important station in the network besides the village. It was the terminus of short turn-offs to the poultry yard, the gardener's house, and an abandoned arbor in a deserted spot.

The main line, Villa-Billiard Room, was the most popular. It was made up of many stations, not to mention the tunnel (you lowered your head to show you were passing under it). The boys especially liked it because it led to unexplored lands. To be sure, the garden around the villa was varied enough: the pond was an inland sea; the greenhouse, with its thick plants and its humid heat, was a kind of Canada, and the fish pond was an important estuary. But there was always the same sand, and these paths going off at right angles, and the villa that was always in sight; it was no better than the suburbs of the villa; whereas over there, toward the billiard room, was the park, and the unknown, and the foreign. You followed paths bordered by flowering shrubs whose hot, sweetened perfume was overwhelming (you opened your mouth to receive it, like a piece of candy). You stopped at a little station at the edge of a sun-devoured pampa. Then the express hurtled across immense shuddering forests and, as soon as the billiard room was in sight, you really had the feeling that you were approaching a great sluggish city full of luxury and calm; one of those colonial cities where, beneath the tall, quiet, and evergreen trees, people with soft voices have nothing to do all day except be happy. It was the city where the Bamboo Song takes place. But then you had to cross, beneath a piercing sun, a huge desert without cities and without stations; then you followed the service-tree path: a new country, with box-tree borders, and little red fruits (poisonous) spread throughout the lawn and the sand. Then another forested region opened up—the enchanted grove—and a turn-off led the train to the shore of a great lake (a trough that was always full) where the locomotive quenched its thirst. And now, en route to the great industrial center on the other side of the world, you again found all the familiar things of civilization, but bigger and more imposing under this new sky. It's quite a sight, then: the express pulling into the huge dark station, whistling without interruption and giving off waterfalls of steam!

It's such a pleasant line that Marcel and Arthur decide the number of trains provided for in the rules is insufficient. Often, either as an "excursion train" or an "inspection locomotive," they cover all or part of the trip individually. And the country of branches, flowers and water that surrounds the billiard room is so beautiful that the locomotives forget to say "chugga-chugga" and to whistle. One time they almost had a terrible collision.

And one day Arthur had an inspiration: "Why don't we use the little dogs from the villa as passengers?" And so it was done. The little terrier, Sourik, the two King Charles spaniels, Gypsy and Lily, who chew on their teats, and Toto, were transported free of charge several times a day from the villa to the pond, from the pond to the fish-pond, and from the villa to the stable. They were even given tourist tickets for the whole network. One train brought them, another brought them back. Sourik, on the gardener's lap, trembled as he waited for the express to the villa. And one day, they left Toto on a set of shelves in the billiard room.

And the trains making local stops on their way to Thiers continued to pass by at the edge of the park. All around Arthur, Marcel and Françoise, the world dispatched its trains and steamships. New lines were inaugurated, and new ports. Cities exchanged their inhabitants. Someone from Puy-Guillaume had gone, just for fun, all the way to Holland!

Oh well, they had to be like everyone else. They had to respond to the world's activity with a continually expanding activity of their own. A crazy plan was born: connect a regular service with the Thiers line—the *real* one. For that they would have had to cross the whole park, which is on a slope. The downhill trains would be easy to drive, but the ones that had to climb back up would cause a lot of trouble. However, one line was started and continued far into the interior, up to the Horrible Tree Station, completely in the wilderness. They led one of the dogs, Lily, there, put her at the foot of the horrible tree, and pretended to abandon her. (She couldn't have cared less, as long as she didn't have to walk any more.) But the return was deplorable. Lily fell out of the rolling chair and pretended she had hurt herself. They had to carry her, furious and slobbering, back to the villa, and all day long she looked at the children with the indignation and terror of a princess who has been brutalized by a mob.

For the next few days they tried to resume service in that direction. But soon the Horrible Tree Station was a station like Trottoir-de-Bouricos (in Bordeaux), where the train stops only once a year.

Chapter 3: The Desert Isle

AT THE BEGINNING of this new vacation the children decided not to bother with railroads any more.

"We've already done enough of that: they work, that's enough," says Arthur.

"And they weren't real trains," says Marcel. "They were chairs. We'd have to have real rails, real locomotives, and real cars. They make them. I saw them in an arcade in Paris. But they're too expensive: Papa would never let us."

"You just don't know how to go about it," says Françoise. "I could talk him into it."

"Oh yeah, Baby? And by the way," says Marcel, "you were lying, Arthur, when you told me that Canada is a hot country with Negroes."

"I never said that!"

"I know where Canada is now. And I know all about history. And all the capitals. What's the capital of Persia? And Afghanistan? And Beluchistan?"

"Teheran. Kabul. Kelat. And what's the capital of Mabulistan? You flunk! I know my history, and geography, too!"

"I have an idea," says Marcel. "We'll go discover a desert isle. We'll plant our flag there. We'll make it into a kingdom, and we'll settle it."

"I'd rather play shipwreck," says Françoise.

But Marcel sticks to his idea. He acts as if he is making up the details as he goes along, but it's obvious that he has carefully thought out everything that he says. The desert isle will be the smallest clump of trees in the garden, which is a little bit off to the side and triangular. The plants will be considered the inhabitants of the isle....

"But then it isn't deserted," objects Arthur.

"No: it's savage. And from the moment we get there, it will be civilized."

The little pear trees will be the major cities. The currant bushes and the raspberry bushes are counties. These two little leaves along the ground, big as confetti, are a farm on the slope of a hill. We will explain the borders of pinks and strawberry bushes by saying that "the density of the population on the coastline is considerable."

They begin. The flag is planted. The kingdom is founded. The pear tree in the middle will be the capital; what a big city! All these fluttering leaves, all these budding fruits: it's another Paris.

But they need a king. No, a queen. They think about the princesses they like the best. Arthur vacillates between Blanche of Castile, who is so good and so beautiful, and Anne of Beaujeu, whose hairdo is a big cone full of candies. Françoise prefers Mary Stuart, because she knows a song about her. But Marcel is in love with Anne of Bretagne, quite simply because she is Breton, and because Bretagne is the favorite little sister of France.

"Mary Stuart!"

"Blanche of Castile!"

"Anne of Bretagne!"

"No," says Arthur. "This is stupid. They don't exist. We need a living queen. Françoise, come here and let me annoint you! Pay attention. With this vanilla cream, I proclaim you queen. With this balm of my heart, I declare you queen. With this slap that I give you, I hail you queen. That's it: Long live Françoise the First!"

("How smart Arthur is," thinks Marcel, humiliated. "I would have never thought of vanilla cream." When the teacher talked about holy chrism, Marcel had thought of cream, but is was such a perfect cream that it was pronounced "chrism" and spelled funny so that you could tell the difference.)

"I want to be the Supreme Commander," says Marcel.

"Me too," says Arthur. "But, since there can't be two Supreme Commanders, we will be two great commanders. Françoise, dub us knights. I'll show you how. We bend our knees in front of you. You raise us up, you kiss us on the left cheek, once. Then we turn our backs, and you give us each a very little kick."

It was done. Arthur and Marcel feel themselves turn into knights and great commanders. Soon they will be historical figures. It is a great responsibility. And they look in amazement at their Queen. Just a minute ago, she was simply little Françoise, with her big straw hat, her big rosy cheeks, her brown hair ribbon, and the rusted golden anchor on the sleeve of her sailor suit. And now she's a queen, but the gold anchor hasn't started sparkling as if it had become new again. It's almost unbelievable!

Chapter 4: The Reign of Françoise the First

FIRST THE ADMINISTRATION of the realm is established. The Queen will reside in her capital, or nearby. The extremities of the island are placed under the jurisdiction of the two great commanders. Arthur will have the two angles that turn toward the garden; Marcel, the angle that faces the villa. It's a matter of maintaining peace in the interior, destroying harmful insects, and protecting the isle against any aggression from the outside.

And, in fact, here comes Valentine, the Saint Bernard, wagging his tail. The little dogs follow him. It's a pirate with his fleet. The coastlines are readied for defense. Valentine, faced with these threatening gestures, stops, surprised.

"The enemy hesitates," cries the Queen. "Fire!"

And the artillery opens fire on the enemy. Valentine, hit by a clump of dirt that shatters all over his beautiful coat, walks slowly away and goes to stretch out in the shade of the villa.

"We've wounded him," says Marcel.

Valentine looks at the children with an indulgent sadness, rests his snout on his paw, and closes his eyes.

"Let's make peace with him," says Arthur. "Come, Tin-tin, come big doggie."

"He isn't moving. He's mad," says Marcel. "It's your fault, Françoise."

"I won't stand for anyone questioning my orders," says the Queen. "Commanders, go get the pirate Valentine, and bring him back, dead or alive!"

Chapter 5: Revolt of the Great Commanders

THE GREAT COMMANDERS cross the sea to go get Valentine. But Valentine refuses to follow them. Even when they pull on his collar, they can't make him budge a quarter of an inch. And when Arthur tried to grab him by the front paws, he dared to growl.

"Great commanders, why haven't you brought me the pirate Valentine?"

"What if he bites us?"

"Too bad! I told you, I want the pirate Valentine."

"As for me, I say, tough!" cries Arthur. "We aren't going to obey a puppet any more. Marcel, let's revolt. Let's invade the island. Go ahead, puppet, defend yourself."

It is agreed that any territory occupied by force remains in the hands of the conqueror. First the two rebels attack together and, always finding Françoise in front of them, are pushed back to the sea. But they finally separate and invade the island from both ends. Incapable of resisting the attack, the Queen retreats little by little to the center, losing one city, then another, and finally shutting herself up in her capital.

"Surrender!" shouts Arthur.

She refuses. And suddenly she makes a victorious sally, abandons the capital and, recapturing two cities, establishes herself firmly on the extreme tip of the island. But an expedition she makes to retake her capital fails; and she is lucky to be able to retreat to the currant bush peninsula. The dinner bell rings. An armistice is signed.

Before bedtime, with a map of the island drawn up by Marcel, the bases of a treaty are laid. The island is divided into three independent States. The southern tip becomes Françoise's kingdom. The north and the center are divided into two kingdoms for Arthur and Marcel. The former capital is demoted to a county seat. Three cities are elevated to the rank of capital. They will make....

"It's nine o'clock, children."

The three sovereigns go to bed.

Chapter 6: The Peaceful Island

THE NEXT DAY the three sovereigns moved into their kingdoms. A wheelbarrow full of bricks served to outline the interior borders and to fortify several points along the coast. They proceeded to a census of the population and the administration of justice. A slug was condemned to death and executed. They then busied themselves with the various kinds of produce of each State. Marcel's and Arthur's contained all kinds of grasses, and even dandelions. But Françoise's was completely different, and it was easy to see that it was in the south. There were bushes there: currant bushes whose fruit was so abundant that it looked as if, beneath the ragged clothes of its leaves, it had fallen prey to some inner fire. There was also a plant with large wavy green and mauve leaves, with a flower that looked like a big red velvet ear; and negligent rosebushes that let their petals drop all around them. The war hadn't ravaged the island much; the pear trees had barely lost any fruit.

Arthur paid an official visit to Marcel, and the two of them went to greet Françoise in her capital. They exchanged presents. The northern kings went back to their kingdoms, feeling sorry that they didn't inhabit a zone where currant bushes grew.

"Let's look for them somewhere else," says Arthur.

And the era of great discoveries began. The six clumps of trees were six continents, discovered one after the other. With the greenhouse, tropical regions were attained. The railroads of the previous century had disappeared without leaving any of their civilization to the new humanity; not even a memory. And one evening, just as the dinner bell rang, the stupefied explorers perceived, foaming in the distance before them like a wild and unknown sea, the cistern in the kitchen garden, reflected in human eyes for the first time!

Chapter 7: Great Discoveries

BUT ALL THIS wasn't the work of a day, or even a week. Each continent was explored from top to bottom. The closest ones, which were separated from the island by only one bay, presented a semblance of civilization. Their coasts were sufficiently inhabited. There were even a few cities. But the interior was nothing but a vast meadow. For leagues and leagues they walked through high grasses—for naturally they pretended that they were very small, on the same scale as the clump-of-trees continent.

Other parts of the world offered more variety. The parsley patch was a big country of light greenery, caressed by endless breezes. Elsewhere, in the midst of a vast desert, they discovered a half-dozen fat kings with completely round yellow bodies, sitting right on the sand. Big green parasols barely sheltered their enormous rotundity, and since they couldn't move, their subjects fed them by means of an ingenious network of thick green cables, all hairy and cool to the touch.

On the fifth continent to be discovered, one of the

farthest from the island, with a coastline that seemed to be inhabited, they found, at a five days' journey into the interior, an immense city made of identical dome-shaped glass palaces, all in a line. This city was so lovely that the explorers yelped and felt rewarded for all their effort. But the burst of sunlight on the domes of glass was so painful to their eyes that, for fear of becoming blind, they left without entering the city and went back to their ships.

After they had doubled a cape, they disembarked and set off into a region covered with tall bluish vegetation, so light and tangled that it seemed to be the work of a race of spiders. It was the realm of asparagus plants, then at the height of their grandeur, and a continuous festival was being celebrated there. The whole jumble of branches and vines was decorated with a multitude of little red, green, and white lanterns. The white ones were drops of rain that had been taken prisoner, and the explorers liberated a great number of them by blowing on them.

And the ships came back to the ports of the triangular island laden with strange fruits from other climes. They had even discovered a kind of white currant.

Maritime enterprises were established. The distant ports where the ships landed were taken over by the different civilized countries, and the tribes living near the ports asked protection from the monarchs of the island. This was the origin of the colonies. Arthur soon had them in all the corners of the world, and Marcel followed his example. An ambassador was sent to the countries of the Fat Kings, and, without any protestations on their part, they joined Françoise's protectorate.

To identify themselves, and to avoid disputes, it was agreed that each of the three States would plant its flag in the ports and lands that belonged to it. Mommy supplied the necessary pieces of cloth, and Françoise sewed the flags. Hers was red and white, Arthur's was green and mauve, and Marcel's was yellow and blue. When they were planted, it really was a handsome sight; and when the ships passed, they saluted them with three cannon shots.

Chapter 8: War on the Island

BECAUSE MARCEL forgot to salute an Arthurian flag, Arthur declared war on him. But Marcel had signed a secret treaty with Françoise. After a brief campaign, it was all over: Arthur's kingdom was invaded and his capital taken.

"Now you have to surrender to us," says Marcel.

"Never! Fight to the death! I'm going to my colony on the continent over there, and I'm taking the whole thing for myself. I'm planting my flag there. Attack me if you dare, you bunch of cowards!"

"Since that's the way it is," says Marcel, "I'm taking the other continent. Françoise will have the whole island, and so we'll each have one of our own."

Thus man expanded his domain, thus civilization spread across the face of the earth.

Chapter 9: New Discoveries

HOWEVER, there were still many regions left to explore. The sixth continent hadn't even been sighted by the navigators. And once the peace treaty was signed, the expeditions started up again.

One day Marcel discovered the inland sea, the pond. He wanted it all to himself, and that almost caused an all-out war. After many negotiations it was agreed that the main port (the flight of steps going down into the water) belonged to him. Then he settled down there and spent hours exploring the waters of that mysterious sea. On the surface floated those insects that are made up of a horizontal line carried on six thin legs. Maybe they are penmanship strokes that escaped from the school workbooks. They really know their measuring system, and never fail to apply it. Even when they're being chased, they don't forget to count the inches they cover across the surface of the water. They are invulnerable and probably immortal. It's no use raising a tempest around them to drown them. While you're shaking your stick in an eddy of mud, their whole clan is already on the other side of the pond, busy measuring the calm section of water that's left.

And further on, exactly where the sun plays at balancing its big flashing vibrations, a ballet of little round animals, like bubbles, turns and flickers. In vain do you try to upset them: they pass between the knots of the landing net and, without wasting a moment, start up their little ballet somewhere else. And if you keep bothering them, just when you think they are going to fly away, they dive, and disappear into the bottom of the pond like a handful of black seeds.

What strange animals there must be at the bottom of the pond! Marcel turns pale when he thinks about it. All that life hidden in the mud, in the slimy coolness of the sleeping water, terrifies him. He imagines that he, too, is living among these animals in the green hair of the seaweed, and it makes him feel queasy. He doesn't dare stir up the whole bottom of the pond; he still doesn't dare to bring his landing net back up to the water's surface. He's afraid of seeing what shouldn't be seen. It's more than enough that, once, an olive he remembers having thrown into the pond the year before, had risen back up to the light, alive, and armed with two little hand-like fins. He was going to grab it, but the olive was too heavy for the two little fins: it tipped over, and disappeared into the depths.

But sometimes temptation is stronger than fear. That's how it is today. This pile of rotting leaves that he brings up from the bottom—why not examine it? Just now, look, one of the leaves looks like it moved. And, turning it over, you see that it has three pairs of legs. Marcel understands the history behind it: a leaf had fallen, still green, into the pond, its veins had turned into legs, and it had kept on living. And along the rim of the pond, right there in the sunlight, the leaf walked just like an animal! Marcel had thrown it back into the water, shuddering. It wasn't right for such a thing to be exposed in broad daylight. He realized that he mustn't speak of it to anyone. Anyway, who would have believed him? It was like the white train; a secret between the pond and him. The water was inhabited by dead creatures to which it actually gave new life, a cold, mute life, a dreamlike life. And the sun of the water, with its pallor, its endless agitation, its great white streaks of light; that was what he had heard about one evening at the dinner-table when there was company: *The sun of the dead.*

A scary dream that he had that night kept him away from the pond for a long time. And the next day, Sunday, on a long expedition, he discovered the sixth continent. A few miles from the coast, black, immense, and high as a mountain, began the virgin forest.

Chapter 10: The Virgin Forest Is Inhabited

It wasn't wise to tackle it; anyway, vines blocked his passage. Marcel decided to circumvent the forest. By following its border he was bound to get somewhere. He walked for a long time, at least a minute and a half in grown-ups' time. He even began to wonder if the expedition would run out of supplies on the way back, when he finally reached the end of the forest. He heard voices. And there, at the corner, "an unexpected sight," as they say in real travelers' accounts: "an unexpected sight met his eyes." Two human beings were sitting at the edge of the forest, on the shady side, and a dog was sleeping at their feet. Two heads of long, red hair falling on their shoulders; and their arms, covered with a completely white kind of dress; two pairs of blue eyes, big, surprised, wild and tender; two white faces with little round mouths and slightly elongated chins. It was too much! If there hadn't been more than one red head of hair, one pair of blue eyes, he could have kept his composure. But before this double beauty and double sweetness, alive, breathtaking, meticulous, there was nothing to do but beat a hasty retreat. The retreat turned into a rout, and an out-of-breath Marcel came running back to his kingdom.

"Arthur, the virgin forest is inhabited."

"I don't care!"

"Arthur, I saw two savage queens and an animal asleep at their feet."

"Explain!"

"All right: there are two girls sitting on the other side of the peapatch, and they have a dog with them."

"Two carrot-tops?"

"Yes...." says Marcel, hesitant and slightly shocked. It's the first time he's heard the expression "carrot-top."

"I know; it's the two little Matous, the new worker's daughters. They live in the park. Their father is a strong-minded man, according to Papa. Yes, he has bad ideas; like a real vagabond. He says he won't have anything to do with the steward or the boss...or your father, outside the job. And he tells horrible tales about the bosses. I bet they didn't even say hello to you."

Marcel is truly astonished. It's true: they didn't say hello to him. He would have thought, rather, that it was up to him, if he had dared, to bow deeply before the two savage queens. Vagabonds are beggars who are always ragged and dirty and have messy hair. And Marcel remembers seeing Matou, the worker, almost as well-dressed as the steward. And Madame Matou, a strong, red-headed woman, doesn't look at all like a female vagabond.

And those girls, well, they are better dressed than Françoise!

Chapter 11: Negotiations

THE NEXT MORNING, Marcel tries to sound casual:

"Hey, Arthur, how about asking the two *Matous* to play with us?"

(He knows they are there, right nearby, and he would really like to bring them to visit his kingdom and tell them about the deserts, the forests, and the mysteries of the sleeping water. He thought about them for a long time last night before he fell asleep.)

"Oh!" says Arthur. "I don't think they like to play. The oldest one is almost thirteen."

"That doesn't matter. Ask them anyway."

Arthur calls to the two little Matou girls.

"Would you like to play with us?"

But, without saying anything, they shake their heads no.

"I told you so, Marcel. Anyway, you know we don't play with the workers' children."

"Why not? Is it because we don't want to, or they don't want to?"

"Oh, both," says Arthur, looking at the tips of his shoes.

"Papa says it's better like that."

"Wait. I'm going to ask them. Say, would you like to play with us?"

The two heads shake again.

"Let's go," says Marcel suddenly. "Arthur, let's declare war on Françoise. There's a port on her island that I want."

Chapter 12: Something Better Forgotten

"They refused because they're shy," thinks Marcel. He really wants to believe it. "It's shyness."

The next morning he had succeeded in convincing himself. And he decided to make a third attempt.

"They don't dare...." And yet, they came back to sit right nearby, behind the pea-patch, and they are perfectly comfortable. You can hear them chatting, but the way you hear pigeons chatting on the roof, without making out any of the words. Ah! They're calling their dog. It's through their dog, a good-looking French pointer, that Marcel planned to win them. He approaches and calls the dog himself, the way he calls Sourik:

"Come here this instant!"

The dog doesn't come, but he stops, pricks his ears and waits for Marcel.

"Leave him alone; he doesn't know you," says the biggest of the little Matous. And the youngest cries:

"Finaud! Here, Finaud!"

"Finaud, come here this instant!" repeats Marcel, and he approaches, holding out his hand.

Finaud, wagging his tail briskly, leans his muzzle toward the outstretched hand and, dashing suddenly, seizes Marcel's arm.

"Finaud! Here, Finaud!" shouts the little Matou.

The dog releases Marcel.

Marcel was brave. He succeeded in hiding his fear and he made, all in all, an honorable retreat, with a threatening gesture at the departing dog. But behind him he hears this:

"We warned him. He deserved it."

"Oh!" He has to hurry back to the house because his cheeks have already turned pale and his chin won't stop trembling. He finally reaches his room, locks himself in, and lets his tears flow. Fate, look what you have done: a man is crying, you've caught him off guard, all he can do is cry for the rest of his days. It isn't Finaud's bite that hurts. He wishes it would bleed, but it doesn't bleed. There isn't even a tear in his sleeve. It will turn blue and, in three days, brown, and next week there will be nothing there. And it isn't his wounded pride that hurts so much. Oh! It's the rejected friendship, the warmth that no one wanted. Oh! I came, offering all my heart, and the dog bit me, and they said, "He deserved it."

Now Marcel understands Matou's bad ideas. They really *are* bad: neither pure cod-liver oil, nor magnesia in your orange marmalade, nor castor oil in your black coffee could be as bad. "Child of the bosses, you won't play with the children of the workers!" These were Matou's ideas. And they hadn't even asked, "Did the dog hurt you, Monsieur?" But his maid, if she had been there, would have fainted when she saw Finaud jumping on him. His father would have had the dog killed on the spot. *They* said, "He deserved it!"

Marcel, a little calmer, dreams of vengeance. First he swears to devote his entire existence to persecuting workers in general and Matou in particular. He will begin as soon as his eyes aren't so red. He will complain to his father, and demand that he fire Matou and that Finaud be killed. He knows very well that he will do nothing of the sort; but it makes him feel better to think about it, to imagine the meeting with his father and Matou's humiliation, the execution of Finaud and the tears of the two savage queens. No! He will cause them no pain. His vengeance: that they guess that he has cried. Still not enough; he starts all over again. Too bad they can't see him; too bad Finaud didn't bite off a big hunk of his flesh.

Now, dry your eyes: you're beginning to cry on purpose. Instead, look for a name for your unhappiness and for its cause: child of the bosses, you won't play with the children of the workers.... And Marcel remembers having heard his father say, after a boring explanation:

"It's what the (a very long name that ends in *ists*) call: the Iron Law of Wages."

Chapter 13: Joan of Arc, Murat, and the Black Prince

THE RAINS COME at the same time as the September sun, and the garden, island, and continents are locked up in a big silver cage that the wind swirls endlessly around. No one can go out anymore. Arthur is furious. But Marcel, who has known more bitter disappointments, is resigned. Standing next to the window, he watches the rain fall. The pathways turn into seas and oceans. "The sand is happy," thinks Marcel. "This reminds it of its river." All the same, it's boring not to be able to go out and get a little wet, because now is the time to brave the elements and go kiss Mother Nature on her suntanned, streaming cheeks, to get drenched with her smell, and chew on her warm, moist tresses. Marcel would like to be, at this moment, on that hill in the park, a distant, hard-to-reach region where his friends, the pines, are. Those pines with their red bark are the Indians of the trees. It's easy to see by the way they set themselves apart, and by the steep places that they choose for setting up camp. It's obvious that they are nomads and outlaws. They must take advantage of the bad weather to relax a little while men are kept shut up in their houses. They must hold some grand council and smoke the peace pipe—Marcel once saw the smoke—and listen to speeches by the elders of the tribe. The rain is scattered by their solemn proceedings, and it doesn't penetrate their camp. Their beautiful floor, made of red needles, always stays dry and slippery. Here and there a lovely frail green plant that they decided to protect—some daughter of the white men found in the desert—plays and bends graciously at their feet. However, they plan and prepare their expedition for next winter, and tell each other in sign language how, hidden under coats of snow, they will go down the hill and chase polar animals on the icy pond. The thought of winter fills them with an obscure joy, which they express by making a darker shadow under their branches.

It's still raining. Marcel tries to imagine the effects the rain would produce if it lasted for eight more days. No doubt the pond would overflow, and you would see goldfish wandering about in the garden pathways. And all the strange animals of the pond: the live olive, the leaf; perhaps others, even bigger—birds turned into fish, with thick black, cold wings. And those tin soldiers whose vessel sank last year, what happened to them? Would the abyss give them back to him, discolored, corroded....?

Hey, there's an idea! An idea that is born and surges before him like Pallas in arms. The soldiers! The six boxes bought during the last trip to Paris from the magician with the blue beret in his basement on the Rue de Dunkerque. Marcel goes to look for them and empties them onto the big table in his room.

"They're all flat," says Françoise, disappointed.

Yes, they are all flat. But soon you get used to their flatness. Their colors are pretty, their uniforms precise. A wounded knight falls, his knees bent. Napoleon, hand in his vest, surveys the field of battle. There are battles from the Hundred Years' War and from the Empire. The notion of time is abolished by decree, and the children decide that the French of Austerlitz will fight against the English of Agincourt.

But the main thing is to continue the wars begun in the garden. This way it will be a war among the three heroes, and, when it stops raining, they'll divide up the conquered territory and revise the map of the world. Everyone chooses his army and his leaders: Arthur will take the English led by the Black Prince: here he comes, visor down, and so black that he's practically blue. Françoise picks Joan of Arc astride a white charger: she's dressed in silver armor that makes her sparkle like a fish; she has her banner in her hand, and she sallies forth with her head uncovered, more blonde than words can express. And no doubt Marcel will take Napoleon?

"No, that's too ordinary," he says, and Napoleon (tough luck!) is exiled to the top shelf of a distant wardrobe.

"I'll take Murat," says Marcel, introducing the king of Naples to the Black Prince and Joan of Arc.

And here comes Murat, in crimson boots, white pants, a green coat trimmed with fur, and a hat shadowed by immense tricolored plumes.

The introductions are barely over when war is declared. Everything is put to use: an old fort, building blocks, a doll house. The Black Prince, at the head of an Anglo-Russian army, goes to fight against Joan of Arc and her knights. She is repelled in a first encounter, but Murat gallantly comes to her aid with an army made up of French soldiers from different centuries. The campaign continues, with mixed successes and setbacks for the allies. The projectiles are sometimes pennies, sometimes exploding bee-bees. The pennies endanger the porcelain vases and the windows, and the bee-bees cover the furniture with dust and sand, filling the room with smoke. But there's no getting around it: this is war with its endless stream of horrors!

Chapter 14: The Three Hundred Years' War

So Marcel dedicates himself totally to war. Conquer or die. Life has denied us the satisfactions of the heart, satisfactions which we thought were our birthright. It's better this way: we will demand from glory and power pleasures that are less pure but more violent. And the pennies mow down the ranks of the infantry, and the bee-bees explode.

New taxes are already necessary. The three countries are in danger, and demand volunteers. Piggy-banks are broken, Papa is asked for 10 francs, and the children write to the magician on the Rue de Dunkerque. The war expands: more than 1,500 men are lined up. The war fleets (old boats from previous years, repainted gray) are readied, and a break in the weather allows for a big naval battle on the pond.

But everything goes badly for the two allies. One of Françoise's last baby teeth is wiggling and hurting. Distracted and sulky, she makes mistakes, and a string hangs from her mouth. From time to time, between battles, she goes up to her ally or to Arthur, hands one of them the end of the string, and says:

"Pull a little bit. Not too hard!"

But since she holds the string, it's a mere formality without appreciable results, even though she screams as if someone had torn out a piece of her jaw. Preoccupied with her tooth, she defends herself poorly; her soldiers are taken, her ships sink or are set on fire by Arthur's firebrands. It's so bad that Marcel, reinforced by a shipment from the magician, declares war against her and is obliged to forge a new alliance with Arthur.

One against two, that's good! And even better now that we have the Rue de Dunkerque behind us. Marcel hands over to his enemies all the soldiers that have already arrived, except for the French ones, who will join a new army that's on its way. He signs a shameful treaty that he knows to be only temporary, and, reduced to a small piece of territory on the edge of the virgin forest, he prepares for new battles.

"It's funny," he says. "We haven't seen the queen...the carrot-tops?"

"And there's a good chance that we'll never see them again," says Arthur, in a decisive tone. So decisive that Marcel doesn't pursue the matter, and looks toward the sunset and toward the depot where the magician's package will be left tomorrow....

Chapter 15: France at Bay

War is declared once again. Marcel's ambassador, the little dog Sourik, is the one who transmitted the declaration to Gypsy and Toto, the ambassadors for Françoise and Arthur. This was done according to all the rules of diplomacy. Sourik was brought before the two ambassadors; there, with one paw raised, just like a lion on a crest, he slapped Gypsy and Toto in the face, one after the other. The three animals look at each other:

"What will they think of next!"

And Sourik apologized for his brutality.

"As you can see, they're holding me by the paw."

And on the big table Marcel's army displayed itself opposite its enemies' armies. It is a grave moment: France, invaded from all sides by a Chinese fleet threatening the coasts of the Vendée and a Norwegian army landing at New Caledonia, staves off attacks from all points.

But now the disasters begin. All the colonies are attacked at the same time. And even the savages declare war against France. There are battles on all the tables, on the mantelpieces, any place where two soldiers can stand,

and fleets collide and catch fire in the waters of the reservoir.

Marcel loses three battles marshalled between his breakfast and lunch, a naval combat before his afternoon snack, and two cities in the evening. Arthur doesn't know where to put all the prisoners he's taken.

"If Françoise didn't have her tooth, I'd finish you off," he says to Marcel.

And Marcel starts another big battle.

"Oh!" cries Françoise in the middle of the fight, "That's it! I pulled too hard, and it came out!"

"What?"

"My tooth." She shows her pulled tooth at the end of the string. And since it's bleeding a little she opens her mouth, closes her eyes, and lets out a huge wail.

Chapter 16: France Victorious

ARTHUR GRABS his sister's tooth and throws it in the middle of the French army, roaring: "Fight to the death!" But Marcel lowers the tricolored flag, hoists the white flag, and sends a truce-bearer to announce to Arthur's headquarters that he surrenders unconditionally. And soon afterwards he signs a treaty that reduces France to 17 provinces plus Noirmoutiers Island.

He collects his thoughts, meditates and, to prepare his revenge, he assembles his generals around him.

Because now a whole nation surrounds him, and at the head of this nation are the generals and their great leader. The first leaders disappeared a long time ago. Joan of Arc was captured and burned at Lausanne by the Swiss. The Black Prince sank with his torpedoed flagship. And it's been so long now that no one can remember exactly how Murat died.

New times have produced new men. On Arthur's side a new leader by the name of Arthur the First, then his son Arthur the Second, succeeded the Black Prince. By the same token Françoise had Françoise the First, Second, and Third. With Marcel, great families successively held power; a breed of men that were strict, hard on themselves, full of (some say devoured by) ambition, and born to lead. Marcel sees them coming from afar (after their sortie out of their box); he follows their careers or, rather, directs them; grants or refuses his sympathy. They all start out with exploratory journeys. With them Marcel rediscovers the park. They go beyond the Horrible Tree. Little by little they reach the great meadows, the willow-grove, the big oak tree, the little pond with its three islands, and the mysterious region filled with the hoarse soliloquy of the water in the red basins. A young lieutenant, Armèze, crosses the big pond in a sailboat, and a lieutenant colonel, D'Auzambert, reaches the high land of the pines.

But, before them, how many had failed! How many were drowned in the two pools, how many perished in the rapids of the watercress bed! And, in the end, the ones who survived are given the honor of being fired upon by Arthur's artillery. Arthur aims well and strikes hard. A penny thrown at headquarters mutilates more than one body, tears off more than one head. A new triage is made, and Marcel resists the temptation to cheat: that is, to expose the ones he doesn't like and protect the ones he likes. Never mind, fate will decide. And the favorites aren't spared. Armèze, having passed through all the ranks, has finally become the Supreme Commander, old, bent, with a broken leg, half his body chipped off by the flames of the fire-brands. Arthur will quickly finish him off. But a young D'Auzambert is blazing a trail of glory down there in the willow grove.

So, after the defeat, Marcel assembles his generals and asks them what needs to be done. They reply that Armèze's decrepitude is the cause of all their problems, and that they need a young leader. Then Armèze rises painfully: "Messieurs," he says, "so be it. I give up my power." But Marcellic law doesn't allow a leader to abdicate. Before he can be replaced, he must die. "I will die, then," replies the magnanimous Armèze. "In a quarter of an hour I will have ceased to live. But to repay the sacrifice I am making for my country, grant me the power to name my own successor, the great leader who will lead us to victory." "Granted." "Then, oh general, I name sub-lieutenant D'Auzambert generalissimo of the French armies, and I bid you adieu." And the heroic Armèze throws himself into the flame of a candle, which quickly transforms him into a little tear of lead.

D'Auzambert is placed at the head of the army. War is once again declared. Marcel concentrates on aiming well, learns to line up his troops better, and does so well that, moving from victory to victory, France recaptures all her provinces. All the while, at the other end of the world, a young lieutenant Armèze, member of the Indochinese sharpshooters, fights so well against Arthur's Chinese that a new French colony is formed: county seat Peking, sub-prefects Fuchow, Canton....

Chapter 17: Where It Is Learned Why the Savage Queens Disappeared

AT THE dinner table. Marcel. Papa. Mother. Lead-Head. Lead-Head is a great industrialist, a friend and customer of Papa. Marcel calls him Lead-Head simply because he resembles the sticks of lead in pencils. To explain this resemblance to grown-ups, you would have to say that this gentleman always has gray suits, gray ties, gray hats (maybe he's in semi-mourning?) and that his eyes are gray, his hair is gray—the deep, shiny gray of graphite. But there's something else and, in child's language, Lead-Head is Lead-Head *because*.

Papa is telling a story:

Two weeks ago one of our workers left under rather curious circumstances. We didn't have him here for very long...someone named...Jean Matou. As you know, my factory is open to the public, and during the summer there are a good number of visitors. So it happens that a woman.... "A Russian or Englishwoman" my steward said...asks...about two weeks ago...to visit the factory.

We sent a foreman around with her. She was a chatterbox, and perhaps not very familiar with the subtleties of our language. Anyway, she stopped in front of each bench, and asked the foreman:

"And what is this one doing? And what is that one doing?"

Matou was grumbling in his corner and, when she came up to him, he looked her up and down, disapprovingly, with his turned-up chin, and before she could say a word he said to her:

"*That one* will not see what *this one* is doing."

"Why?" asks the foreigner.

"Because *this one* doesn't want to show *that one* what *this one* is doing."

The foreign lady didn't understand. So my Matou started all over again:

"*This one* doesn't want to show *that one*...."

"Trade secrets?" said the foreign lady, going away. It certainly didn't bother her to be called "that one," and that's what Matou got for all his trouble. And the other workers made fun of him. Matou, furious, leaves the shop, goes into the steward's office, throws his apron on the desk, and says that he won't spend one more hour in this joint, where you are exposed to insults of the bourgeoisie, and if the others can stand it, he can't!

The steward...asks him to lower his voice. He retorts by giving him a summary of the communist doctrines, the bit about the "boss's dog," and the foreman arrives just in time to prevent them from going at each others' throats. Naturally, that evening he went to see the paymaster, and the next day he moved out—he lived in one of the small houses in the woods—with his family. He went back to his home town, which is...the mining district of this province.

"How stupid," says Mother, "to lose your job for such a childish thing!"

"Oh," says Papa, "Matou didn't have any trouble getting a new job."

"That's what politics does for you!" says Lead-Head. "What did he want to be called: Monsignor or Your Majesty? Politics...."

"I would say, rather, that it's a question of *domestic* politics," says Papa. "Yes, the true cause of that scene and of the departure of Jean Matou was...female jealousy. Their wives had pitted them against each other. The steward and Matou, yes. You see, Madame Matou "looked too good," the little Matous—I saw those two kids near here, with a lovely pointer—were better dressed than the steward's children. So...one of them had to go. I was sorry to lose Matou, but I couldn't sacrifice the steward for him."

Chapter 18: The Birth of an Empire

AND WAR starts up again. Encouraged by his initial successes, Marcel takes the offensive against Arthur. But the strength of all his arms and his diplomacy go toward separating Françoise from her alliance with Arthur.

Françoise wants two Basque dolls that were brought back last season from Biarritz, and who have been staring each other down for four months on a shelf in the drawing room.

"If you stay neutral," Marcel tells her, "I'll give you the lady. If you switch to my side, I'll give you both of them."

Françoise hesitates, but ends up taking the whole deal. It will be a princely wedding, and the diplomats get to work on it (although it doesn't seem to amuse either Sourik or the King Charles spaniels). The ceremony is performed with great pomp. You could call it a marriage of convenience: Françoise is marrying Marcel, whom she doesn't love and who doesn't love her, but who is buying her; while she is bringing him Sweden, Germany, Austria, and two or three small countries as a dowry.

Marcel, at the height of his power, has a twinge of sadness: Ah! He would have much preferred marrying one of the savage queens, even if she had nothing for a dowry but her blue eyes and red hair!.... Then again, if he wasn't sure that he would never see them again, he would never have agreed to this marriage.

But now the cannons roar, stifling the voice of regret. A Franco-Prussian army, having taken Constantinople and Moscow, marches toward Peking across the Siberian plains. The armies and all the fleets flee before the triumphant march of the Armèzes and the D'Auzamberts. Little by little, Arthur loses all his soldiers, and one by one his great leaders are taken prisoner. He already has an Arthur XXIII leading his troops. However, his aim is still as deadly as ever: one of the window panes in the library bears witness to this, and one of the D'Auzamberts and his honor guard were sliced in half in their own headquarters.

Arthur has only two hundred soldiers left.... Now he only has one hundred soldiers. And late one afternoon at the end of September, Arthur has only one champion left: to be more precise, his last great leader and an escort of six Belgian lancers.

The little group sets out across the field of battle, and Arthur XXIII throws himself at the feet of Armèze V, who spares his life, and even creates an imaginary kingdom where he will be honorary king.

A great victory is celebrated. (The little dogs, afraid they will be forced to participate, disappear under the furniture.) Music of every sort is performed, from Japanese music, which has red pants with white stripes, to savage music, which is completely naked. Universal peace is declared, and Armèze, under the name of Armèze the First, is elected emperor of The Whole Garden. The honor guard stands in formation in front of the palace (the doll house) above which the all-blue international flag is raised; and finally the Emperor, standing on his tortoise Rosalie, is presented for his people to contemplate.... And Marcel feels the need to go tell the whole garden about his triumph. He goes out into the golden warmth. But how funny everything looks this evening! Someone must have been playing up there, too, and left the sky in a mess. It's down here, close by, mixed up with the earth. The sky is full of mountains thrown one on top of the other. A promontory, looking like the bow of a big iron-clad ship, pierces an ocean of gold. Some high cliffs are punctuated with interminable cannons. At the ends of the cannons shines a purple ocean. Some other mountains are long, flat, and pointed, like certain seaweeds; and others are porous, and behind them there are tournaments of unknown suns. Still others guard more distant horizons, all black and crowned with terror, that make you think of these words: The Ten Commandments. Even the air around Marcel is full of strange things: faces that are geometrically constructed with stretches of light and rays of sun. The house, the lawn and Marcel on the lawn are in the middle of the sky and, at the depths of an abyss, Valentine, stretched out as if he were sleeping, waves his lovely white plume twice in honor of the young master.

And Marcel, who has come down to the garden, notices that he's walking among the things of heaven. A sunbeam visits the triangular island, from where civilization once spread throughout the rest of the world. He surprises three sunbeams leaning against the cypresses that guard the basin. One sunbeam is still sleeping stretched across the alley, and Marcel turns away so that he won't disturb it. Others venture into the thickness of the virgin forest. And there's one scaling the wall.

Marcel contemplates his empire, built up piece by piece with so much toil. A great era is coming to an end with this vacation. He thinks about his great leaders, who henceforth will be called emperors. Naturally, he will bring them with him to school. He'll find some place to put them. But he wonders if these future emperors will be as heroic as their predecessors, who were all great leaders!.... Oh! The immortal sacrifice of Armèze the Great! Oh! The man who first stood on the edge of the iron-clad vessel where the water sings in the language of the Underwater People!.... Oh! the soldier who spent a whole night in the middle of the pond, exposed to sea monsters, standing, sword in hand, on a water-lily leaf....

Epilogue

THE OLD LANDAU groans, but gently, politely, without losing any of its dignity as "the master's coach." It's a climb. The horses walk. It's hot in the closed landau. Papa and Mother occupy the back seat, and Marcel and Françoise are sitting opposite them. (They are bringing Françoise as far as town, to amuse her a little and to keep Marcel happy while the suitcases are being packed.)

"Are you asleep, Marcel?" says Mother. No answer.

"Hey, Marcel, you asleep?" says Papa.

"Yes, I'm asleep!" shouts Marcel, and he opens his eyes. He didn't want to open them for five minutes so he could see if he had guessed exactly where they were. He closes them again and starts counting five times sixty seconds. Will his parents keep getting involved in what concerns him and doesn't concern them for the rest of his life? At least at school he'll be left alone. He is happy enough to leave home. He's looking forward to school.

Where are we? We must be crossing the little village that tries to follow the road but gives up very quickly. The sound of the forge blesses us as we pass by. We leave behind the cattle bells of a tip-cart. We pass under a cool archway with branches that brush against us and grab the coachman's whip for a moment. Then the red light under his closed eyelids tells Marcel that we are once again in the fields in the open sun.

He thinks about his past vacation. He thinks about the way it has just ended. Arthur, who stayed home, said to him:

"Well, good-bye, Monsieur Marcel."

"Why are you calling me Monsieur?"

"Oh, really! Now that you're going to school in Paris you are going to be a monsieur, and I will call you Monsieur; Papa says it's better that way."

Marcel didn't say anything. But he remembered the Iron Law of Wages. Rejected again! Before, he would have taken these signs of deference as an homage well due his merits. But now he knows. "Son of the bosses...." And now he sees everything in a different light. There was never any real equality between him and the two steward's children. They don't play with him: they entertain him, which is not at all the same thing. And if they are entertaining him, who's to say that he doesn't bore them? He remembers how Françoise pretended to be afraid when they passed the Horrible Tree. And Arthur surely lost all his battles on purpose, in the end; he had had enough. Surely when "the boss's son" isn't there, Françoise and Arthur don't play the same games. Maybe they even make fun of him because he is afraid of certain trees, and because of the games he makes up. Ah! And is it true that he is going to become a monsieur, like Papa's friends, like Lead-Head? All the monsieurs look alike, and the sight of them is enough to overwhelm Marcel with boredom. He wonders if they aren't going to betray him and make a monsieur out of him behind his back. After all, maybe it's fun. You wear a flower in your buttonhole, you smoke fat cigars with bands around them and you say: "That's all politics is good for." But why must he then leave the good faces that he knows and loves? Blaisot, the gardener's son, friend of those winter vigils (he's in the regiment) and Jean, the coachman who knows how to make cages, and Marie Bargarin, the oldest worker's daughter? Ah, no—they aren't all alike. And Marcel knows them so well that, watching them from behind, at a distance, he could tell what they were thinking about.

They pass over the local railroad tracks (more friends). They will soon be in the little town where they stop to eat lunch and rest the horses. Hey, how about pretending that the owner of the Hotel de France is an Indian chief and we are explorers?

...They climb back into the carriage; and they leave that little town sulking in its boredom in the sun. Marcel plays at closing his eyes again and, after a long time, saying "We are here," and looking to see if he guessed right. Ah! He didn't guess right: this is only the Sleeping House. But opening his eyes he sees that Papa, Mother, and Françoise all have their eyes closed. This is the time to keep his eyes wide open.

A big sunset sky, full of long clouds, invites him to travel among its continents and islands. It's God himself who welcomes him and opens his big Sunday up wide for him. And Marcel, without embarrassment, goes to sit on God's lap, and looks with him at the pictures that he traces one by one across the sky.

"Lord God, your sky is really pretty, and your earth isn't bad, either."

But something still hurts him deep inside, and he says:

"They pushed me away, God. The dog bit me, and they said, 'He deserved it.' And, just now, Arthur called me Monsieur. Anyway, tough! I won't love anyone anymore."

And God answers with his pictures, his pink clouds with gold fringes, and his big silver meadows.

"Go ahead, love anyway. And you know, it's like this: to love anyway is what makes real love. I, too...you will learn later.... But if they still push you away, and if they chase you away everywhere, come to me. I don't reject anyone."

This is said with the rending of an immense gray wasteland, and the silent collapse of a pale gold waterfall.

Marcel looks and understands. But in the farthest room in the palace of his thought, the beautiful blind demon, Despair, turns away without saying a word.

Rachel Frutiger

To Marcel Ray

WHEN MY MOTHER used to tell me about her school years in Geneva, and about her friends there, Penelope Craigie and Rachel Frutiger, I could only picture my mother as I knew her then, walking with other women under the trees of Jean-Jacques Island between the two big white bridges and the blue water. It wasn't until much later, on a summer day during the cantonal fast, when I was crossing Plainpalais, that I realized she had been talking about little girls. And I pictured them like the ones I used to see, satchels on their back and two pigtails over the satchels, walking by twos and by threes and by fours, and holding each other's arms when they cross the busy streets. I knew who "those two little French girls" were; the two brown pigtails: my mother; the two blonde pigtails: my Aunt Jane. And I followed a path into the center of town that must have led to their school. But does it still exist? It was called "The School of the Good Shepherd," or maybe even "...of the Good Shepherds." Naturally, it was "the best there was," and Madame, our Director, used to say, referring to my grandfather:

"It's just like these haughty French—who else would

think of sending his daughters to the most aristocratic day-school in the city when he can't even make the regular monthly payments!"

How aristocratic this day-school must have been! It certainly must have disappeared, along with so many other aristocratic things. A real little German princess went there; and some very distinguished and ugly English girls, with names like The Honorable Mildred Taylor, for example. And there were three sisters with red hair who spoke a barbaric language, kicked each other under their benches during class, and wore big gold crosses around their necks. A valet accompanied them and stood watch outside the door. They were called "the Prok sisters." During class, when they weren't fighting with each other, they sucked on their gold crosses instead of taking notes. One day a cross came loose and fell on the floor; you could see that it was hollow: a liquid poured out. The supervisor picked it up and, turning to the teacher, she cried:

"Madame, it's ether!"

The Prok sisters turned as red as their hair, and the two women looked at each other for a full minute without saying anything....

I try to picture Penelope Craigie. But one half of her name is a marble bas-relief: Penelope sitting in front of her loom—next to her is a flat little lamp, with three tips lit, to show that it's nighttime. Craigie makes me think of hyperborean mountains. But that's because I know that she was the daughter of the priest at the Scottish chapel in Reykjavik, Iceland. Little Craigie must have been blonde and nervous, with a head the size of your fist, two light gray eyes, and cherry ribbons at the end of her pale pigtails. Even in the winter she went barefoot in leather sandals that were too big. Because of that, and because she came from so far away, and because she must have felt terribly disoriented, and because she was slow of speech, and because all sorts of wonderful accidents occurred in her pronunciation, one of the little French girls, in the secret recesses of her heart, loved her.

Rachel Frutiger was the daughter of a banker who had a large house on Bergues Quay. She was just like any other little girl from Geneva, with the same accent, and she swore by saying, "Good Lord!"

Several days before Christmas, at the end of class, Madame Director beckoned to the two little French girls.

"It's been two weeks now since your father wrote that he was going to send me the money for the last two months. Tell him for me that this bill must be settled before Christmas, last warning."

My grandfather came from an ancient family: he had silver plates and table settings with his coat of arms on them, and a fabulous tric-trac set inlaid with several precious stones. He also held political beliefs; and, due to them, he had been disinherited by his father, imprisoned by the Joint Committees, and, finally, exiled by the Prince-President's government. And so he lived in Geneva among the other exiles. They were the defeated, the victims. But they were also men of a noble generation. In good times and bad they had done extraordinary things that still reverberated throughout Europe. People they didn't know were interested in them, admired them and loved them. My grandfather's special friends were Monsieur Sue and Monsieur Barbès. Once, when Monsieur Sue had to show his passport at German customs on his way back from Bath, one of the customs officers had said to him:

"Euchene Zue? Ze vandering Chew? Fabulous! Ze knife!"

And one day when Monsieur Barbès had gone to "take a look at France" from the frontier post on the Gex road, he came back deeply moved, with a story that he just *had* to tell. He had encountered a wagon train loaded with stones coming from the Jura. In front of him, one of the wagons got stuck in the mud, and the whole train was motionless. The waggoner shouted, the horses pulled; nothing budged. Finally, addressing the lead horse and giving him a tender pat on the nostril, the waggoner had said:

"Come on, old Barbès, give it all you've got!"

And there were saviors of humanity who had founded Fourierist communities in America. And dreamers with unkempt hair who were communists first and Saint-Simonists last, who described the beauty of the society of the future in such a gentle voice, and for such a long time, that you didn't dare lend them less than 20 francs. And those poor Polish refugees. And the Italian conspirators who wanted only enough money to buy a dagger!

This time my grandfather repeated that Madame Director could easily wait, and that the money from France would come early next month. Then he went off to sell his tric-trac set to an antique dealer so he could invite a few friends to Christmas dinner and give a generous donation to the Refugees' Fund.

The day before Christmas, at the end of class, all the students went up to Madame Director's desk and placed a small bouquet and the envelope that their parents had entrusted to them. The two little French girls would have liked to wait until last, but Rachel Frutiger kept on fussing with her books and notebooks.

"All right, young ladies, let's see..." said Madame Director.

The two little French girls burst out at the same time:

"Papa said he will be getting the money from France next month. He said...."

"In other words, you haven't brought anything? Well then, as long as the overdue fees haven't been paid, you will not be allowed to attend classes. Tell your father that for me."

Then Rachel Frutiger came up:

"Madame," she said, "I haven't brought anything, either."

"What, Mademoiselle Frutiger? You?"

"No, Madame. Papa will send you the money after Christmas. Are you coming, you French girls?"

Outside, Rachel was ambushed, grabbed, and pushed against a tree so she couldn't move.

"You did that for us. You have the money!"

"No, I don't! I swear!"

She struggled, and her book bag opened, and with her notebooks out fell an envelope that jingled when it hit the pavement. Rachel Frutiger cried, "Good Lord!" gathered up her books and her envelope, and ran away.

When vacation had ended, and the money from France

hadn't come, and because they didn't want to upset Papa, they pretended to go to class. They left with their book bags on their backs. They spent an hour touching up the snowman that had been built at Plainpalais Square. But after that, what was there to do? They didn't dare walk through the center of town for fear of being seen by one of their fellow students. One day they tried to take the back streets to Rhône Street, to take a look at the knife with the twenty-five blades displayed in a shop window. But Penelope was standing right next to the cutlery shop. And after a long walk through the alleyways, the little French girls began to lose heart.

They couldn't stay in Plainpalais, either: they risked running into Papa or Mother at any moment. So they turned off into the suburbs, following long sad streets along the Arve River or toward Carouge. They held each other's hands. They got tired quickly. And they felt as if danger surrounded them. They had some terrifying encounters.

Once a worker with a belly full of beer found a temporary support in the middle of the causeway. He ventured to stretch out his arms and, when he saw that he didn't fall, he started lecturing passionately, in a severe voice. Women passed, looking the other way. But this was something new to the little French girls, so they stopped and looked at him. Then he addressed them personally, threatened to come closer, and his voice followed them for a long time, attracting the attention of passers-by. A little farther on, some little boys scared them by shouting as the girls went by. Other boys came up and talked to them. One of them even dared to pull one of the blonde braids, the way you pull a bell-rope. That earned him a slap. But the moment of triumph was short-lived: they continued their flight immediately; a retreat through the snow, like Napoleon's retreat from Russia. Surprise and suspicion followed the school children who were seen in the streets when everyone else was in class. And one evening the maid said to Mother:

"It's funny how dirty these young ladies have been getting at school lately."

By now they were used to spending their days without lessons or homework; classes had already been forgotten; something else had begun. The book bags that they carried on their backs no longer served any purpose; they were nothing but an added weight to their fatigue, a taunt added to their feeling of defeat. They walked straight ahead without seeing anything. The only clear thought in their numbed brains was the time: to get home at the right time, as if they had just come back from school.

One day they came upon a sort of portal, half-open, at the end of a dead-end street. They crossed a courtyard between some abandoned buildings and found themselves facing an immense Dutch door, yawning in the shadows. They went in. It was a hall of immense proportions. A sort of dock, like you see at a port, dominated the background. They climbed a few stairs to get up and, at one of the ends, they walked down a plank. They felt sheltered there, as if they were in a fortress on a hill overlooking a plain or the sea. If you leaned your head backwards, you could see the beams and the other parts of the framework, interlacing in the shadows where spider webs trembled. As soon as they got up the nerve to talk out loud, the children began to explore the domain they had just discovered; and were frightened when they suddenly saw two eyes staring at them between the boxes and the barrels, near the ground. It was a cat, which got startled in turn when they clapped their hands.

It took them a while to notice that there was a little room above the entranceway, and that a miller's ladder leaning on the edge of the dock led to the door. It seemed as if the ladder had been brought and placed there after they had walked into the room, so astonished were they that they hadn't seen it before. After a moment's hesitation they didn't resist the urge to see what was in the room, and they began climbing the ladder. But the spaces in between the rungs made them dizzy, and they were secretly afraid of the abandoned room. They hadn't climbed halfway up the ladder when they realized that night was falling, climbed back down, and ran till they reached the first streets of Plainpalais.

For two days they looked for the dead end and the big door. It was a place where you could hide and rest; it was also a great place for races or for playing war. And that unknown room, above the hall, just like the sky over the earth.... On the third day, they found the dead end. But the big door was closed, and they found a sign: *For rent; contact....* So they began their walks through the suburbs again. The snow melted into mud. Nauseating, cold, and vile smells rose from piles of sweepings and gutters, and got under their skin. They quickened their pace and stopped talking. How many months did this existence last? Exactly eleven days.

At the end of that time Monsieur Sue came back again from England. True, he spent time on the Continent, but he left so much of himself in England that you always had the feeling that he was only passing through when he was anywhere else. Monsieur Sue kept a mannequin modeled after his own body with his tailor in London; a molding of each of his feet with his shoemaker in London; and with his hatter in London, a thing without a name that was a mold of his head. Monsieur Sue arrived as he must have left: with his hair well curled and the frill of his shirt well pleated. He sat down, a little hunched over, and crossed his lovely hands over his crossed knees. He was shy, and spoke little. He was sad. But it was not because he had once been expelled from the Jockey Club, or because he had seen his novels in the hands of the lower middle class, with which he had nothing in common. It was simply that he was growing old, and casting a shadow on the sidewalk of Pall Mall that was somewhat less slender than it used to be.

Separated from the world as he was by his princely upbringing, and by a civility whose secret has forever been lost, it was amazing to see that Monsieur Sue was interested in the details of daily life. Now, he immediately noticed that the children were unhappy; he brought them into the garden and made them confess everything. The next day, the little French girls were again seen in the Classes of the Excellent Shepherds.

Childhood, clean and white, with your well-combed hair, your little bare feet in sandals, Geneva's sweetness, young souls perfumed with saintly virtues, I've often thought of you while thumbing through my mother's

Holy Bible and her collection of Hymns with the black binding and the Swiss Cross imprinted on it. I have often thought of telling you what I just wrote. I imagine that the sad music of the Hymns and your inner life were secretly joined. Rachel Frutiger, who loved love, you must have preferred the one that tenderly sings:

Nearer, my Lord, nearer....

But the most beautiful of all the hymns is the one that has this verse as its refrain:

Abide with us, Lord, abide with us.

Summer Homework

To Marcelle Jeanniot

We bought nice new paper to make clean copies, and pens (a whole box), and a ruler and a big eraser, soft and friendly; and an envelope full of sheets of thick blotting-paper: pink, light blue, green, violet. And a box of twelve colored pencils, and tracing paper, to make postcards. We had gone out early to buy all this at the stores near the Louvre, the day before our departure. Unfortunately our credit was limited, and we couldn't buy that lovely box of forty colored pencils that we had wanted for so long, or we would have had to deny ourselves all the other things we needed. Anyway, a box of forty colored pencils is something for grown-ups, "ideal for architects" or for engineers. And we had to leave all those desk accessories, invented to satisfy the writer's slightest whim, after looking at them for such a long time that it seemed that they had already begun to belong to us. Later, when we are a college graduate, or a Ph.D., or even—who knows—an author....

How beautiful that morning at the end of July was! A big fresh breeze carried the smells and noises of the Rue de Rivoli to the stationery store shelves. The clear morning came in through the arcades; the length of the sidewalk's edge shimmered, still damp, while the grandiose shadow of the palace covered the humid pavement; but the shadow stopped a little further down at the edge of the Palais-Royal Square, which opened itself wide like a big pale gold living room. Someone had emptied a box of brand new soldiers and lined them up on the sidewalk in front of the Ministry of Finance. At the end of all the arcades, near the wooded avenues and the gardens with golden lattice-work, Monsieur Sadi-Carnot was finishing his lunch. Now he walked into his study. Someone undoubtedly put fresh sheets of blotting paper in his writing pad every morning, and as soon as he had signed a decree, someone put a new pen in his pen-holder. On his desk you would certainly find all these charming crystal objects, these perfect jars of glue, these racks of pen-holders, and they must have designed a big case of 100 colored pencils especially for him.

Still, with twelve *deluxe* colored pencils you can make some awfully nice cards. How hard we were going to work! How carefully we would prepare our summer homework assignments! Every subject would be studied in depth, and for that we would not be satisfied with the elementary manuals that we used in school, but would research the questions in the upper-class texts, and even in original works, like Saint-Beuve's "Monday Chats." Then we would re-copy these assignments without a single mistake, leaving two margins on each sheet, one on the right and one on the left, like in books. And when classes started again, our new teacher would see right away that he was dealing with an excellent student.

Actually, during the year that just ended, we weren't as good a student as in previous years; in fact, we were just average. But now it was summer vacation, and because we were going to be free, and since nothing was demanded of us, we were going to work with all our heart. This first day of vacation was already so lovely, with errands in cabs that increased our feeling of freedom, and lunch at "Chez Foyot" surrounded by older boys who had just passed their baccalaureate, this last day in Paris before the silence of the country filled us with a perfect joy, and we inclined naturally toward study. We were so overwhelmed with freedom and pleasure that we instinctively sought out the supreme pleasure, which consists of the pure, detached activity of the mind. And, in the study plan that we set out, the summer assignments were only one episode, the way a series of articles commissioned by a magazine would be for a poet. We were resolutely going to surpass the limits of the school assignments, and see what was beyond. They must have been hiding something from us: all these textbooks, excerpts, "Selections." We wanted finally to see the great works in the original.

Farewell, Saint-Germain l'Auxerrois, little patches of blue-black stones and gentle blue sky; farewell, lovely fresh wind that has chosen to spend all its summers on the Colonnade lawn.... We would make lists of these "basic works" to which we were always referred by notes on the bottoms of the pages of our cardboard-covered textbooks; Mommsen on Roman history, for example, and "The Face of the Earth" for geology and physical geography. Our parents would certainly agree to buy them for us. And if need be, we would give up some toys, an excursion, or even that all-white bathing suit we'd been dreaming about during evening lessons as early as June. (Here is the old, boring, and sublime facade of the French Institute, where, at the rate we're going, we will certainly enter one day. And here's the sharp turn and the breeze from the Rue de Mazarine.... Which door do you use to get into the Institute?) Yes, we must begin by reading one of the authors whose thought dominates the entire modern intellectual movement, like Bacon, or Descartes, or Kant. It would be a good initiation. We would then possess a key that would open the individual apartments of each of the women who, like Cherubin's godmother, are "beautiful, but imposing": the Sciences. Once we had really penetrated the doctrine of one of these great minds, all the rest would be easy for us, and we would have a tremendous advantage over all the other students. "Discourse on Method".... Once we possessed a method, *the* Method....

But we had read or heard that Leibnitz in some way had improved on Descartes, and we knew that his "Monadology" is a slim volume, nicely printed in Hachette's collection of classics. In fact, we were about to pass the Hachette Bookstore. A few words to Mother (who is next to us in the cab—we had forgotten about her), and, five minutes later, we are the owner of "Monadology." It's a good choice: Leibnitz' name is less known than Descartes'. We only have to be seen carrying one of his books for people to look upon us as an extremely studious young man, maybe even a future scholar. Oh! We are going to become a very distinguished "monadologist!"

It's really too bad that the only homework we have to do in natural history is in botany. Otherwise we would have gone to spend a pleasant moment in Eyloff's store on Monsieur-le-Prince Street, where in past years we bought, and especially—alas—looked at, so many rock fragments, so many beautiful crystals, so many ammonites and belemnites; and on pieces of coal, imprints of ferns, and palm trunks; and then, right afterwards, "the moderns": all the gems of a great entomological collection. Fortunately next year will be zoology, and we'll be able to prepare by reading The Encyclopedia of Natural Sciences, for example, or even the Systema Naturae by Linnaeus. Alas, those are works we have heard of, but no "young student" has ever managed to get a glimpse of. Anyway, as long as we didn't have an in-depth knowledge of our Monadology, it would be better to abstain from reading long books.

We were going to start studying right away. No; tomorrow, on the train. Today let's watch the streets pass, streets that we won't see again until it's time to go back to school, when autumn days, overwhelmed with glory, are already parading in full regalia down the Champs-Elysées.

Mother has an errand to do before our lunch at Montrouge, so we're off in the old, slow, echoey carriage through the city where everything is as clear as the style of a good writer. We can leave our serious mind and relax a moment in the contemplation of noble views. However, we would have really liked to go take a turn around the Botanical Gardens, say good-bye to the hippopotamuses, and bring (this is an old scheme) a little ice cream to the white bear, who must be suffering at the bottom of his cement ditch. At least we would enjoy taking a moment this afternoon to pay a last visit to the Turtle Republic, that is, Potel & Chabot's window at the Palais-Royal, where, in a countryside of rocks, sand, and water, you can see a whole crowd of land turtles, the only inhabitants of the country. They come in all sizes; but the most remarkable are two mothers, fatter than human brains, who spend most of their time sleeping, heads and paws pulled into their horny armor, motionless and shut up like stores on Sunday. But in the meantime we are going to see, once again, the distant land at the shaded, sheltered end of the Boulevard Saint-Michel where the sleeping lion reigns. Here we are passing back by the jack factory, with its black facade that has some bizarre objects, which must be jacks, painted on it. A little further on will be "The Soldier of the Earth," whose plaque inspired deep reflection "during our childhood" two years ago, when we still wore the short vest of primary school and the white, turned-down collar.

But what with the long lunch and the other errands that Mother had to run, we couldn't even see the Turtle Republic. We got home late and, tired as we were, we had to walk up the three flights of stairs because the elevator was sick.

We couldn't sleep.

The sight of the package containing the stationery purchased at the Louvre that morning reminded us of our summer homework and our study plans. From tonight on, our vacation began in earnest, and we wanted to watch it begin. Tomorrow: the departure, the trip, lunch in the train's dining car, and an attentive reading of "Monadology"...Nothing will distract us from our studies. They will be the main thing in our life, and the rest—little incidents, little pleasures, games, even sentimental adventures—will be nothing but pastimes to which we won't be able to abandon ourselves completely. We will seize them, given the opportunity, but without attaching any importance to them, and we will enjoy them without afterthought. And if they fail or disappoint us, it won't bother us, because our true *raison d'être* will be our studies. Moreover, our studies won't take us away from the deep feeling, the great friendship of over a year that fulfills our existence. On the contrary, study and friendship—a passionate friendship like ours—are of the same nature. There's no way to explain this, but it's true. The more we work, the closer we feel to our beloved friend. Oh secret passion, so pure, so faithful, so tender, and so furious! Grown-ups will never know of it; no word could make them understand these things, because it's not a friendship like theirs. But now that we're alone, and it's nighttime, let's say our friend's name out loud.... That's enough. We will never name him in front of our parents, or in front of anyone. As that friend of Mother's sang the other evening at the piano:

Cut me, burn me, I'll never tell:
I'll keep my secret, and keep it well.

...Study, friendship, and peace. We'll be at peace, because we know our friend is at the seaside with his family. In school we were always fearful. Our friend is so light-headed, so imprudent; and compliments, flattery, presents, and even a brutal boldness, have so much power over him! It seems as if he purposely tries to make us unhappy. But no, he wouldn't dream of that: he plays, hides behind trees, jumps over a railing, runs across the lawn, runs into a thicket, lets us catch up with him, receives and gives a kiss, and then goes back to the place where we were waiting for him, and says laughingly, "What's wrong with you?" Or else we spend hours doing nothing but following his glances, and spying on his gestures and activities, and we break every rule to follow his footsteps, and see where he's going. Oh! and our friend's betrayals, and the bad things he says about us, and his mockery, and his false promises "on his mother's head," and that horrible threat, never to speak to us again, that makes us such a coward that we agree to look the other way.... All that is over.... for two months. Our friend is with his sisters, under his guardian angel's wing. We will write him and give him good advice, and because he's very sweet and eager to please, he will admit that we're right and reform his behavior. Yes, he is very sweet, but there's also something violent and wild in him that nothing can touch. Incomprehensible friend.... He is lazy, but he is also very obedient, and respectful of authority, and he defers so well to the teachers' desires that he is the one they almost always pick to recite prayers. And yet it sometimes seems that they know how flighty and undisciplined he is, deep down.... Beautiful fruit, secretly spoiled.... Dear God, make him be good! Holy Virgin, whom he loves so much, watch over him!

We should have started work the evening that we arrived. But first we had to renew our acquaintance with the house, and revisit all those things that speak to us of a distant time, of vacations past, of study days before school, and of loves before friendship. We certainly had to go wake up our bedroom (we awakened it with a start—the floor cracked so loudly that we shuddered). We listened one more time to the long story of the wind in rooms that didn't get used to us again right away, and we rediscovered, in the marble veins of the mantelpiece, the narrow Face, which looked at us sadly and reproachfully. We had almost forgotten it; but it remembers everything, and it began telling us about our last summer vacation, and the ones before that, and of winters "back then" with their colds and infusions, their New Year's presents, their scent of oranges and taste of candied chestnuts; and toys that were new; and little dogs that are dead; and long journeys with Mungo Park and Captain Grant's children, and games with the local children; with Jolly Maria, whom we tortured at the end of the day in the hallway; with grey-eyed Francine, Sneaky Francine who was seventeen and who made us look for her scapular.

The face also talked about the woods, and reminded us of those abandoned quarries that we had discovered one morning far away from the house, in the depths of a valley where the river, so big that we could scarcely recognize it, lit up the whole countryside, and where an ancient road—the traces of man, a lost civilization—faded slowly, slowly. Who knows? Perhaps there was an entire village shrouded for thousands of years in the forest.... But certainly the Negro village, Timbuktu, was still there under the high trees of the forest: the four big anthills whose somber domes you came upon suddenly at a turn in the path.

It was too late in the day for us to set out now. But the next morning, as soon as the sun touched the house's threshold, we opened the door and walked slowly down the lawn stairs, astonished by the silence of the fields and the simplicity of the sky.

At the edge of a motionless little black brook that no pathway led to and that you discover by accident, suddenly, in a fold of thickets where it's nothing but a reflection of leaves piled up against the sky, we finally found solitude. Without question we were so happy to be on vacation because we were back with our family. Could it have been otherwise? But a good part of our happiness also came from having found a little solitude. Then why, when we were at the house, did we avoid staying alone with our parents for a long time? Why were we afraid of letting ourselves go on with stories about school? Was it because we had learned our lesson from the experiences of past disappointments? In the funny papers you see jokes about "enfants terribles;" why were there never any jokes about terrible parents? Maybe it's because they really are *too* terrible. But there's another thing: little by little you give up trying to make yourself understood. We have so many memories of life at school that have nothing in common with our parents' memories. It seems that *they* have forgotten everything about *their* childhood.... And little by little we perceived that the part of our existence, already ancient, when we lived in front of them, near them, on their laps, was almost as foreign to them as our life at school was. Their version is different from ours. It's as if they didn't know us. They tell strangers stories about our early childhood in which we find none of our memories. They malign us. It's as if sometimes they even took children's words out of books and attributed them to us. This embarrasses us in front of other people, but since we are very cowardly, we laugh at ourselves with the grown-ups. Luckily, one thought that we keep to ourselves consoles and avenges us: *They haven't seen the Face.*

Just when, tired of our errands, we were going to get to work; that is, to exchange the solitude of the woods for the solitude of our bedroom, our older cousin Mathieu came to spend a few days at the house.

"This book here—Leibnitz—is it yours? You're going into tenth grade and you're already working on philosophy? You're not going to understand a word of it, pal. Here, take the racquets, and let's go!"

And we had actually read "Monadology" twice and we didn't understand very much of it. We should have had a commentary on this work. Discouragement had overcome us. It really was true that you have to take your classes one by one, that there wasn't any way of skipping the program of secondary studies, and that, despite the best will in the world, you have to go one step at a time. The sight of "Monadology" made us blush, and we hid it deep inside a drawer in the library.

But soon preparations for the trip to La Bourboule began.... Where did this joy come from that we felt whenever we left the house? We loved our parents, and they were certainly better than most parents. And they were well-brought-up parents. (Who will ever write the book that remains to be written on "Badly-Brought-Up Parents?") Yes, and why did we always feel a pang of grief when we found ourselves back at the house? Everything seemed so lovely, so luxurious, outside the house. Even the bouillon in railway restaurants, which Papa called "infamous," seemed to taste much better than the bouillon served at home. These were certainly bad feelings, which we should have suppressed....

Naturally, we had to rediscover La Bourboule, its white main steet next to a stream; its park, whose every path is followed by a little clear and noisy brook; and its green hill spotted with black rocks, like a miniature mountain, but nevertheless high enough that people walking up there looked like dwarves from the bottom. We had once made it into a separate country, called the Hill of the Dwarves.

Then for a few days we felt as if we had fallen in love with our table neighbors in the hotel restaurant: two little foreigners with golden red braids, tan and pink cheeks, and very short skirts. All evening they used to play badminton in the hotel garden, counting the blows of the racquet in loud voices so that, to keep from hearing them, we learned to count to sixteen in a language that was possibly English, possibly Swedish, we don't exactly know. This lasted until the casino's Children's Ball, when we danced with Solange, the daughter of that countess who was so friendly and cheery. Then we forgot about the northern beauties to become the slave of the gentle smile and the clear French eyes. But Mother didn't like to see us play with Solange, and she barely responded to the countess' greeting. She even refused to let us get in that lady's carriage to go have a snack on the lawn of the Mirabeau Salon with Solange. We had heard people in the hotel saying about Solange and her mother: "No one goes near them," and Mother, to whom we turned for an explanation, replied:

"My darling, that woman is not a real lady."

Was Solange, then, "not a real little girl?" We'll never know. She was tall, a bit pale, and blonde, with hair so fine that when we danced with her, the slightest breath of air would push a few hairs against our face, and it was like suddenly brushing against a spider web on a path in the woods. She talked like a grown-up. And one day when we were chatting with her, we caught her smiling behind her fan at some other little boys. That made us turn all red. She realized that we had seen her, and she burst out laughing. So, without saying a word, we abruptly left her. That evening she explained that her mother had allowed her to wear only white, and that even in winter she was always dressed in white. Except that in winter there were dresses and coats of wool, and stockings of silk. From her shoes to the ribbon in her hair, everything was white, except, she said, her garters, which were red and blue. Those were their friend's color, or the color of his stable. She had added: "Mother wears the same kind."

After Solange we loved a little flower vendor who ran barefoot behind the "mineral water drinkers." This was a good resting place for our tenderness because it was absolutely impossible for us to have any kind of relationship with her. To see her two or three times a day, to throw all our change at her, and then to imagine long adventures at the end of which, grown great and powerful, we married her at the Notre Dame or Reims cathedral; that was all we could do for her. It was a convenient love, guaranteed to overcome all kinds of obstacles, which didn't encroach upon another passion that had occupied us since the second day of our arrival at La Bourboule: a passion for flowing water. Considering everything, even our infatuations with the two little badminton players, Solange and the flower vendor were only secondary episodes in our life at La Bourboule, which was filled with an attentive, absorbed, loving study of the little brooks in the park.

Then there was the dream of coming back to our childhood home and finding ourselves once again in the uninterrupted silence of the fields and the woods. Noon passes without commentary. At La Bourboule noon was made of chimes, the silence of the streets, and the multiple contradictory noises of dishes and meals being served in the big bright rooms under the half-closed eyelids of the blinds and fringed tapestries. Here noon is no more than an hour that chimes, gaily down there in the kitchen, and hushed, subtly, in the freshness of the empty living room. We no longer knew what to do. The brook, the walks in the woods, were from a past too recent for us to take pleasure in re-living them. We had grown accustomed to our summer, and it began to seem really long.

It was then that the taste and the need for study came to us suddenly, powerfully, one morning as we woke up. We had recovered use of the pen-holder, paper, and books the way a convalescent recovers the use of senses he had thought lost forever after an operation. We vaguely longed for winter and Paris, and studious days beneath the friendly foreheads of the monuments, in the clamor of the deep streets. We would be best in everything, and our friend would be proud of us. We would do his homework, like last year, when he came and sat next to us in the study and drew puppets in his notebook while we solved his problems. This year he would certainly be better behaved; he would no longer seek from others the help and protection he needed....

In the meantime, to work....

In two days we had done the Latin translation: the letter in which Pliny the Younger describes the city of Como. They were perhaps the best two days that we had during summer vacation. We were alone in our room like a man; and sitting at our table facing the window, we worked with care, our mind alert and clear, approaching the difficulties of the text with ease, without haste, sometimes finding a fortunate interpretation that gave our version an undeniably French sound and an almost modern detachment. From time to time we looked at the fields and the woods that stretched out beneath the window, and there was a pleasant contrast between our intellectual activity and the slow monotonous life of the countryside. We had attained one of the peaks of our life: What more could we desire? When we were thirty, when we were forty, we would come back to spend a few summer months in the old family house, to work in peace on some scholarly undertaking.... We would sit at this same table, and out the window we could see the same scenery. Nothing prevented us from imagining that we were already thirty years old: no one was forcing us to study; our parents had finally given up on watching over us and interfering with our business; we were left alone, and we wished to come here to put the finishing touches on a translation and a commentary on Pliny the Younger's "Letters," which all the scholars in Europe have awaited with curiosity and impatience ever since our early works had attracted their attention.

After the Latin translation we confronted our botany homework. Subject: the Root.

Yes, the root.... We know that there is an important difference between the development of dicotyledon roots and monocotyledon roots; but we have forgotten what this difference consisted of. Little matter, for we are still capable of drawing a nice diagram of a transversal cut in a root, in the theoretical root, where we depict the vascular vessels in red and the vessels of the inner bark in blue. Then we will devote a paragraph to the growth of the root and to the growing area, which is located, not at the tip of the root, but a little above, under the root cap. Then we talked about adventitious roots and root hairs. If we add a few observations on aerial roots (which seemed the most interesting of all) to that, we'll be sure to have done a good botany lesson.

And yet.... We did botany for a whole year, we still know little about it, and we haven't succeeded in getting interested in it. We have never seen the notorious cells that they talk so much about; and we only understand this whole process of plant growth by virtue of an act of faith on our part. Perhaps these things actually work completely differently. Maybe the botany they teach us is a science invented expressly to drill young students' minds. Who knows if even Latin is nothing but a big pedagogical hoax? We sometimes thought that all the monuments of the two classical literatures had perished, and that the texts they made us study were really done by the humanists who pretended to have recovered them, and who reconstructed them, or rather invented all their fragments in a Greek and Latin that they made up. So many important manuscripts that were *seen* in the 16th Century were mysteriously lost afterwards! Maybe they were fakes, and their authors had good reason to make them disappear. The humanists could have invented these texts to amuse themselves: they must be people with a clumsy sense of humor; but it was more likely that they had the education of future generations of young students in mind.

We had the same mistrust for everything that they taught us: this predigested intellectual fodder that they presented nauseated us. And then, after all, we weren't angels who can conceive ideas without the aid of the senses, who can always descend from the abstract to the concrete. The only part of the program that managed to interest us was geology, because we'd had the opportunity to discover Eyloff's store, where we could see, touch, and sometimes even acquire the objects that the textbooks spoke of.

But it wasn't just that. What repelled us most about our studies was the uselessness of our work. We were always practicing and never *doing* anything. And it would have been such fun to do something, it would have been so flattering for us to be allowed to participate, even in a very tiny measure, in what they call the scientific movement! For example, they could have entrusted us with monographs on plants. We would spend the whole year studying one or two common plants in depth, and that would have been the best way for us to enjoy learning elements of botany. We would have gone to the textbooks of our own free will to find the information that we needed. As for French, classical languages, and living languages, they could have had us do the lexicon of one or another writer's language. Our efforts would be compiled in Paris, and the best among them would have the honor of publication. Thus, during our summer vacation, we would receive a pretty, embossed book, brand new, entitled "Lexicon of Racan's Language" by the Esteemed Students of the Ninth Grade of High School X, in Paris; of Louis-le-Grand High School; and of Nancy High School. The names of the best students would appear on a list at the beginning of the book: Principal Collaborators: Messrs...." We would read our name there. Our name, printed in a book!

We did our botany homework, and then we immediately began contemplating the subject of French Composition: "Discuss this statement by Lamartine about La Fontaine...."

Lamartine had the audacity to write that he disapproved of the practice of reading and teaching La Fontaine's fables to children. We were all very pleased to learn this; finally someone was taking our side against the grown-ups. Not only did we have to agree with Lamartine, we had to furnish him with arguments, support him with all our strength, crush the "Fables" with the magnificence of the "Meditations" and the "Reflections." Unfortunately, the argument that the poet presented against the fable-teller was a grown-up argument: La Fontaine's fables were immoral, they tended to dry up children's hearts and spoil their lovely illusions. What did we care about that? The biggest defect in La Fontaine's fables, in our eyes, was their lack of poetry. First of all, we had tremendous difficulty in understanding "the lion," "the dog": What lion? What dog? There were the lions in the zoo; there were dogs that were completely different from each other: Crazy Ding, Brutus the Terror, and little Gypsy, who was "well behaved." And then these animals who made speeches seemed to be concerned with the same things as grown-ups. Were they men disguised as animals, or animals with the passions and ideas of men? In any case, they were not animals; they were given that name, but they didn't show it. It seemed as if the Fable-teller had never watched them. And at the end of the fable, there was a moral; some flat and very prosaic reflection which gave us the impression that everything preceding it was created just to lead to that very point; it was like a kind of theorem: "Prove the following...." And if there had at least been a rhythm we could grasp, a well-marked cadence, repetitions of sounds, the whole lovely dance of rhyme.... But, no; no sooner did the poet seem to take off, when he crashed back down clumsily on a verse that was too short. How could anyone tolerate this sharp little flute solo after the grand organs of Lamartine?

Why hadn't our beautiful romantic champion said all this, adding that he, Alphonse de Lamartine, had infinitely more talent than Jean de La Fontaine? And that, if anyone doubted him, he could put the question to any schoolchild? Why did he dig up this accusation of immorality? It rather made us want to reconcile ourselves to La Fontaine. We were in such a hurry to become men, to stop being supervised, and finally to be taken a little bit seriously, that we wanted nothing more than to have our hearts dry up and our illusions fade. But La Fontaine's immorality was as boring as his poetry. Because even in his most immoral work, in those "Stories" that we had secretly read, he was repulsive, confusing, obscure and, despite all his efforts, not the slightest bit funny.

But...what if we were completely mistaken? What if the truth was that we were still too uneducated, too uncultivated to understand La Fontaine and to experience his poetry? Without a doubt our ears, still badly trained, only liked rhythms that were vulgar and easy to remember, café-concert airs and public-house music; they were incapable of appreciating the delicate nuances of La Fontaine's blank verse. In fact just the other day a friend of Papa's came to the house for lunch. He was a presiding judge on the Court of Appeals, a very well-educated old man who had even published, in Lyons, a book entitled *Miscellaneous Works and Recollections of a Magistrate.* In the evening we went to take a walk through the woods, and, as we were passing the brook, this old man cited the famous verse:

The billow was transparent, just as during the loveliest
[days,

And, to show our knowledge, we hastened to add:

My godmother the carp was taking a thousand strolls
[with her godfather the pike.

Then His Honor had congratulated us, adding, "Ah! La Fontaine! We always go back to him. He is the poet for all ages of life; you can open up his books to any page: everything in them is good."

We had reflected on this citation. We opened our eyes up wide to seek out the poetry in these verses, and we didn't succeed in finding it. "The billow was transparent, just as during the loveliest days...." It was like the pronouncement of a ministerial official. "The billow" was pretentious; "just as during" was clumsy and disgraceful. And then, why was the carp our godmother? Why was the pike the carp's godfather? If a child had thought that up, and stated it during a family meal, he would have been reprimanded, told that he was saying silly things, and maybe even sent to bed. Another thing: wasn't it one of the loveliest days then, since they said, "just as during the loveliest days"? And, finally, where in these verses was the mystery of the water, and those long dark shapes that slide, turn, and slowly disappear? A brook is not an aquarium. And also: why compare these fish to people taking strolls? It was useless, uninteresting, there was even something sad about it.... How much more we preferred those two verses where Lamartine describes a young girl that he met in Florence:

When she takes a step, it's as if space itself
Lights up and expands before such majesty.

Yes, that does it! The old magistrate was right, and we were totally in the wrong not to love La Fontaine, and we would do well to refrain from admitting that we don't like him. Not only were we looking for vulgar rhymes, but we also demanded sentimental inspirations and even sensual images from poetry. Surely the quintessence of poetry was in the "Fables," the fruits of the experience of an artist who didn't begin to write until he had passed his fortieth year: a drop of honey, a grain of incense that gave flavor and perfume to the whole book. Later on, when we have become a man, when we have lived, we will discover in turn this precious honey, and we will know how to savor it. In the meantime, it would be better not to tire ourselves out looking for it. That sums up all our thoughts on this literary question.

So why not write them down? Why not edit an exposition of our reflections (interpolating the episode with the magistrate), transcribe this exposition on a clean sheet of paper, with one copy, to give to the tenth-grade teacher with our other summer homework when we get back to school? What if we tried, for once, to write down what we think? Ah! We know very well that it's impossible! We'd have to take La Fontaine's side against Lamartine, cite the fable of the two friends from Monomotapa, expand a bit on the Fable-teller's "good nature" (that would be very good), and to sum up, remind "The Poet of the Lake" of the respect due his immortal predecessor, who was better than he because he was older, because he belonged to the Glorious Age, and because he was classical.

But it was still true that there are some beautiful verses in La Fontaine. This one, for example:

Malherbe with Racan among the choir of angels....

You can see Malherbe and Racan, two middle-aged men with their beards and wrinkles, dressed in the fashion of their time, among celestial choirs of a thousand dazzling angels with multi-colored wings, like the ones in Italian paintings. These beautiful creatures had made way for the two poets, who brought their lyres and sang the glory of the Most-High in hidden rooms in an eternal Louvre. Below them, in the darkness, groveled the vile crowd of kings and heroes, poor people who don't have the power to live on in men's thoughts.

Oh, irresistible persuasion of poetry, we met you early on: first in the Selected Works, and later in the fat, red and gold volumes of Victor Hugo, Lamartine's volumes, which were bound in blue, in the little white and gold Musset, and finally in the two poor and sad looking books that were Alfred de Vigny and André Chenier.

And now we would certainly be capable of recognizing that voice of poetry wherever it made itself heard. For example, last year during Easter vacation, one day when they let us go out with the servant, we bought a few illustrated newspapers. We were especially concerned with "acting the man," and we had chosen what we thought to be men's newspapers: *Parisian Life, Charivari,* the *Gil Blas* illustrated supplement, *Turn of the Century*.... In the omnibus we held them up so that everyone could see the titles. We were so preoccupied with the effect we were making on the public that we could scarcely understand what we were reading. But then, suddenly, our attention was caught by a poem; we had recognized the voice of poetry, and our heart had responded to it violently and with delight; there in the midst of the licentious pages of the *Gil Blas* illustrated supplement, next to a drawing that would send us before the disciplinary council if it were found in our possession at school, were several stanzas of a sweetness and simplicity so penetrating that it stirred our emotions.

At first, we thought that the poet was mistaken, and that he didn't know his craft very well, since all the rhymes in the first stanza were feminine. But then we saw that all the stanzas had feminine rhymes, and we understood that it was done intentionally, and we decided that it was better that way. After reading it three times in a row, we already knew this little poem by heart, and for several days we had recited it to ourselves in a soft voice. None of the poems that we had read in the Selected Works was as lovely as this one. It was much better than Victor de Laprade, J. Autran, Brizeux, and Chantavoine. But later, when we got back to school, some doubts occurred to us. Didn't this use of feminine rhymes constitute quite a serious breach of the rules of prosody? And didn't this breach greatly diminish the merit of the piece? This would undoubtedly prevent it from being inserted in the Selected Works; it made it a sort of freak, very lovely, but removed from real literature. Moreover, we found it in such bad company, in this forbidden newspaper! Perhaps the author was some lazy young man who had died from living a dissolute life, without even knowing its value. Undoubtedly Arvers' sonnet was far superior to it; undoubtedly Victor de Laprade and J. Autran were much more serious poets, since they took up so much space in the Selected Works, side by side with the most uncontested Classics, and we had been wrong to love that impure and irregular poem. We had bad taste as well as bad feelings and instincts. We didn't love our good parents—who sacrificed themselves for us at every moment—enough, we wanted to rebel every time someone told us we had to love someone or something; and, to top off all this depravity, now we were admiring bad authors.

We had forgotten the name that was at the bottom of the poem in the *Gil Blas* supplement (we had purposely abandoned our newspapers on a bench in the Luxembourg Gardens before going back to the house). But we hadn't forgotten the poem. It started like this:

The serenading men
And their lovely listeners....

And the very fact of thinking of this poem and saying it in a whisper in our room incited us to do evil: we would put off our French compositions till later and write poems. Our memories of La Bourboule left us no peace. They demanded expression, to be set down in a lasting manner. An evening party in the park didn't want its beauty and ardor just to disappear, and it was our mission to prolong it night after night. The Venetian lanterns illuminated the brook until one o'clock in the morning. How beautiful they were among the leafy branches! Especially the ones that were all alone at the edges of the paths or in the heart of the groves. They consumed their anxious and brilliant lives so madly.... Everyone admired them, and feared for them. Sometimes one of the prettiest ones—one that interested us and was like the name Solange among young girls' names, because of the rarity of its colors—suddenly caught fire! And you could see the black flame eat all the flounces in its ballerina's dress. We, too, were like the lanterns at the evening party: the pain and the joy of several loves consumed us. The music floated down the central pathway; the torches of the retreat shook in the wind on the casino porch. From loving so much, and from being so cruel and so loved, perhaps Solange would die....

But little by little, without warning, darkness came where there had been light. Many of the lanterns had already gone out, and others took fright and started trembling. The one farthest away no longer existed; we went to see where it was, and found it asleep and still lukewarm. As the people and the lights disappeared, the voice of the brooks grew bolder and louder. Solange's laugh was mixed in with it. She had left for a shadowy region with Willie and Gaston, and we searched for her in the clamor of the streams.

We would also have to describe, and in nice regular verse, the days at La Bourboule, and the time of day when we left the hotel, as the setting sun threw the mountain's door wide open, and we saw, among inaccessible cliffs, the road that was not made by men. We would have to render the tinkling of the dinners under soft little lights and show, in the ten o'clock-in-the-morning clarity, the dwarves on the march on the back of their hill.

But all this couldn't fit into one poem. Let's first try to describe life at the hotel and the two little foreigners playing badminton in the courtyard....

We devoted a whole day and half a night to it, and at the end of this time we had half a dozen stanzas, each one composed of two verses of nine syllables, one of six, two of nine, and one of six. We took care to place the action in an already distant past. It was a "childhood memory," and one might suppose that the author was a young man of at least sixteen. We had experienced so much since then. There was our stormy liaison with Solange, our passion for the flower vendor, and a long journey back home. Unfortunately, we had wanted to end with a casual touch, and so we used an expression that was so familiar that we wondered if it could be written down. This expression caused a grammatical problem that we couldn't manage to resolve. We said:

Loved I one sister or the other?
I never was certain: Their mother
Always dressed them alike.

In these three lines, there were three feminine rhymes in a row; a serious breach of prosody. But couldn't we consider *"alike"* as an adverb instead of an adjective, and make it into a masculine rhyme? Ah! We hoped so with all our heart, because then our poem would have been absolutely correct, without a single mistake, and maybe even worthy of being included in a collection of Selected Works after our death. Moreover, using verses of nine syllables had been a bold move. This would make our poem a rarity, and might one day make it worthy of being cited as an example in prosody texts.

Encouraged by this success, we were going to tackle other themes. We would also mention the sojourns of past vacations: Luchon, Bride-les-Bains.... Shady groves of Vichy and lawns of Uriage, we would sing your praises in verses of twelve syllables! One day, the way people recall Jean-Jacques at Charmettes, people would think of us at the foot of the Vanoise, on the dampened footbridge that trembles in the eternal cry and the frozen dust of Balandaz. And you, Island-with-Gray-Eyes, Noirmoutiers, at the end of blue pathways, earth and homes amidst villages of sailing ships on calm mornings, do not refuse to inspire your poet!

And, once again, it was a battle with words. Once again they refused to come. And yet we had given them a warm welcome when we met them for the first time in books. The rare ones, bathed in dreams, the ones that designate things with great precision, like the names of parts of a tool, the ones that express an aspect of the weather, or a group of objects like "masting, sails;" we had welcomed them; we had thought, "It's a good thing to know," and we had treasured them in our heart. And now, look how, when we need them, they vanish.... And besides, such a mass of impressions to coordinate and set in motion, it was like trying to stir up the whole surface of a pond with a hoop-stick. In the end, the few words that came to us refused to let themselves be caught up in the gears of rhyme.... So we retreated, powerless, despondent.... And we know the rules of prosody so well! Our first poem, however, was not so bad....

Alas, when we re-read it cold, we saw very well that it didn't express much of what we had wanted to say. It was well-organized enough, and, recited with talent, it would have produced some kind of effect. But on close examination it lacked everything that we called "poetry."

Ah, we really were good for nothing, and Papa and Mother were right when they told us that we would "never amount to anything...." At our age, all children are ugly and disagreeable. We're well aware of it: it's what grown-ups call the ungrateful age. It's the age when we are the most narrow-minded, the most vain, the most silly; and the graces of childhood are beginning to leave us. Then it's as if there is a wall between grown-ups and us. We mistrust them; we don't want to understand any of their ideas. They speak, and in their most serious sentences we manage to find obscene double meanings; they are the innocent souls, while we are the men of pleasure and vice who know life inside-out. We begin to discover that they were making a show of austerity and duty for us, and we pay them back for it. And then we see each of them in his trade, in his rut, with his business and family, and, even more important, with that mysterious thing that they practically never call by name: money. Money: the dangerous and complicated tool that we have neither the right nor the power to use. They are the masters of this tool, and look what they make with it: careers that deform them, businesses that are an affront to the spirit, a family where children like us grow up in subjection, in fear and ignorance of life. We see them, we judge them with the impartiality of pure spirits that have no vested interest in their world. We despise them, we detest them, we envy them. It's easy to understand that they don't find us very likable.

Especially us; we were more shut-off, more "ungrateful," more easily thrown off-guard by grown-ups than most of our schoolmates. They knew how to make people take them seriously. They had flair and confidence, they had a well-defined sense of their social status, and you could tell by looking at them that they came from a good family. But we doubted ourselves so often, we attached so little importance to grown-up conventions, we made so little effort to understand them, that we never even tried to develop relationships with them. To look and listen to us, no one would have believed that we were a rather outstanding student in one of the most famous schools in the capital; and we sometimes even looked exactly like someone from an orphanage in the provinces. Once we had made the little motions of politeness that we had been taught, we withdrew into ourselves, and there was no way to get another word out of us. Even if they spoke to us about the things we liked most, about geology for example, we momentarily forgot all that we knew, and we listened without budging to the stupid remarks of the grown-ups, who were still batting the theory of cataclysms about. As for poetry, we'd never talk about that. It was a secret as serious and as sacred as our friendship.

And yet, sometimes, when we saw how misunderstood we were because of our manners, we tried to improve ourself a little. Then we displayed our science, drawn from school textbooks; or else, knowing the importance that grown-ups attach to the possession of money, we set out to talk about Papa's properties, and our parents' horses, carriages and servants. In the end we carried it off so well that sometimes we seemed like a little pedant, and sometimes like the son of some prosperous shopkeepers. We definitely didn't know how to live. It was enough to make us give up on ourself. And we felt so unhappy that we rushed back to our two shelters: friendship and poetry (by other people). Really, we couldn't live happily without our friend at our side, or else in the imaginary company of the serenading men and their lovely listeners....

In the first mists of autumn, the train brings us back to school. We left without having time to revisit the brook, and we forgot to say goodbye to the Face. The train tramples the horizon, tears up the forest, and shrieks across a veiled, dreamy, and solemn France. Goodbye, countryside: it is sweet, it is sad, too, to leave you. We will dream of you often in the city, where no view looks out on you. We will try to imagine your life under the November sky and in the January snow. If we could come back and surprise you one winter night.... Oh—we forgot something—the box of colored pencils. So what; we'll go buy another box tomorrow morning in the stores near the Louvre. There's something else that we have forgotten, but voluntarily: the two or three summer homework assignments that we were silly enough to do. No one ever hands them in to the teacher, and he doesn't even ask to see them. To hand them in would mean you want to become his favorite student, the "teacher's pet," and that's frowned on by everyone. Certainly if some dummy did them and happened to bring them to school, the other students would grab them, and everyone would chant over and over in a singsong voice, "Nyah, nyah!" Or else the big kids would get involved, and bury the pages according to ceremony. For that, they make a single file and parade through the courtyard, singing:

They buried him in the potter's field
For an unbelievable price
'Way in the back of Père Lachaise....

We'd take part in the procession, and be careful to sing in a booming voice, because we'd sing as a tenth grader.

Memories of our friend make out heart beat faster.... If he were sitting here next to us on the train.... To travel with him, to visit his parts of the country—which is so far away that we have to look at the stamps on his letters, which take a month and a half to come, to understand that he isn't inaccessible and that maybe one day we'll visit him there.... Yes, to meet him again, as a man; to tell him everything we forgot; to rediscover our whole childhood in his smile—which has become even more serious—and to stroll with him in the streets of his native town, which has such a sweet name, and which we dreamed about so much.... To travel forever...to never go back to school...never go back home....

As soon as we left the station, we realized that Paris still hadn't tuned up its noises. It was like listening to an orchestra when the instruments are warming up, one at a time, before the gesture that opens the land of music. In our building we were the first tenants to come back.

We found our bed again; it's softer but narrower than the one at home.... All the same it was nice to be there all alone, safe from the others, whom we'll see again in a few days. Good; we'll see what the new ones look like. Anyway, now that we're in Paris, we're safe. Look how Time has brought us back to the place where it had us start out. It's good. The slowness and regularity of time have their advantages; and you can trust time. And yet, a thought.... What if it were to suddenly break down, like when the spring in a watch breaks and the hands start turning so fast that you can't see them any more? Then you would certainly see mountains cave in like sugar loaves in the rain, and men's lives would be as short as the lives of bees. No, don't worry; listen to its measured steps in the alarm clock....

What is it saying? "Next day, next day, next day?" Or the first name of our friend? Yes! It really looks like it knows.... Ah! Now it's something else: it's saying "A month a-way.... A month a-way...." What? What is going to happen next month? A composition on a Greek theme? Good, watch it speed up its pace, and you can't follow it any more. Let it continue on its journey all alone. It looks like it's hurrying across the entire night, to rejoin the daytime sounds. How did that poem end again? There was the word mandolin.... A chattering mandolin! Ah! Happiness suddenly comes, to find us on the verge of sleep: the day after tomorrow, in the tumult of the first evening back at school, under the red lights, in the dust, at a turn in the hallway, a little brown hand will rest gently on our arm....

Portrait of Eliane at Fourteen

To Jean Royère

It is a very lovely garden. In the middle, an abrupt, tall, leafy mountain of scalloped foliage. It's made up of only two trees—a large black cedar and a tree from Baja California, a marvel, the only one of its kind that anyone has been able to acclimatize to France: a coal-black trunk and, all around, the flutterings and twistings of a thousand branches covered with thick, gentle green leaves, branches that plunge back into the soil of the lawn, that trail along the grass and, higher up, curve into figure eights like a whip that has frozen in mid-air. These two giant creatures with their branches intertwined spread shade and coolness throughout the garden.

It's not very big, but this garden is as beautiful as the gardens of Asia Minor, in the midst of desolate waste-lands. The lawn, with its bamboo draperies, surrounds a deep pool of water that is constantly stirred by the curved jets of the fountain. And a single path, shaded by palm trees, cedars, and nettle trees, winds its way through the grass. A wrought-iron gate clad in ivy, hidden by the laurel hedges, protects the pathway from the clouds of dust that are stirred up from the white streets, and en-closes the garden. In the midst of the bamboo stands the bust of a poet of old Languedoc on a marble column.

Leaving the burning streets, you go in, sit down on a bench sheltered from the Mistral—the blue of the sky seems less harsh through the deep green of the cedar leaves—you listen to the sound of the water. That's because it's a public garden: the shadow of a proprietor never darkens the lawn. But the vagabonds' delicate souls come here to drink their fill of fresh air and shade. The train station is nearby. They burst out of the dusty, smoky tracks and plunge into the calm of the greenery. They go off by themselves. Vagabonds are such experts in the art of going off alone.

But vagabonds are not the only ones who spend time in the park. You'll also find the small-time investors from the town, a few old women, and majestic Catalan wet nurses with their babies. And also the petty bourgeois from the countryside and the hamlets who have come to take care of business in the county seat. Now that all their errands have been attended to, they sit here for hours, idle, thoughts already elsewhere, waiting for the train that will bring them back home. There, among the latter, is Eliane, a child full of daydreams, with her mother and her little brother, who is beginning to walk.

Eliane has been fourteen since February, and it's April now. She is a child. But she's already so big for her age, so plump and strong, that soon her huge silky golden head of hair will no longer land thickly against her shoulders, brushing against her back—and probably in the fall her mother will start dressing her in long skirts. She will blossom in the Midi's southern summer. In the meantime, her youthful vigor, her rustic health, are readily apparent: her firm, rounded legs stretch out her black woolen socks; she can no longer button the sleeves of her blouse around her plump wrists. The dress she is wearing today, masterpiece of a dressmaker from Murviel or Clermont l'Hérault, this "fancy" dress—brownish, with white stripes—is without a doubt her last short dress.

Eliane, silent and all wrapped up in her dreams, looking indifferent and obedient, is sitting in a chair across from her mother, who is knitting. Her mother is a smallish woman, thin and dark, with sharp eyes. A practical woman whose thoughts rarely stray from meals, mending, laundry, and savings. She thinks she understands her daughter, whom she totally dominates with all the authority of the head of the household. But actually she is, like most parents, completely indifferent to her daughter's inner life, and perhaps she doesn't even suspect that people can have inner lives. She has never fallen out of love with her husband, a tall blond with a Germanic head, ferocious looking but with a gentle disposition. He is the only being in the world whose ideas and feelings really matter to her. The little boy who is there, a formless mass wrapped up in white and topped with a flat straw hat, this baby who can barely walk and with whose amusement Eliane is entrusted, is the latest token she has given of this unswerving love—he has his mother's black eyes. Eliane looks like her father: she has the pink and white complexion of daughters of the North, and blue eyes; that's why her mother sometimes exclaims with a sigh, "That's not the kind of daughter I would have chosen, with *those* eyes!" This pronouncement, and many others as well, along with other caprices of maternal tyranny, made her lose this daughter's affection. Eliane is afraid of her mother, and obeys her against her will.

Her mother absorbs, annihilates her, holds her in a thrall which becomes more and more painful as she becomes a "young lady."

When will it all end?

Luckily the door to dreams is open night and day to young Eliane. After all, there must be places to hide from the outside world, and life can't be too hard on a big child with fairy's hair and the deepest, most beautiful eyes in the world. Even up till last year, she herself was a fairy; she visited their palace, just like in the lovely stories in books. And there was Prince Charming, in particular.... Ah! Prince Charming! Eliane had been in love with him.

It was just like the painting of "The Swing": he was seated on the hanging plank holding the two ropes in his hands, and she climbed up next to him; the plank hesitated a moment and then gently, leaning backwards, bending and stretching his legs (whose every curve was molded in blue silk hose), he set the swing in motion. She admired his strength; she felt his presence so strongly that she felt herself getting dizzy; and she had to restrain herself in her bed from crying out in fright. Little by little the movement quickened, Prince Charming carried her above the treetops, glided with her through the air. Rustling leaves trembled before and behind them, the ropes whined, and they burst into the open air. Just then, the swing twisted and they fell, hurled into the depths.

Then Eliane, terrified, clasped Prince Charming's chest, abandoned herself to his strength, and closed her eyes.

It wasn't just the swing; there was the gondola, too, at the Lido; and the Venetian nobleman (who was really Prince Charming) lying at the feet of a beautiful and haughty *dogaressa*. Eliane got in the gondola; she was not angry with the beautiful *dogaressa*: she knelt before Prince Charming and murmured, "I am your humble slave." She had read that somewhere.

And then there was the Naked Man in the Illustrated Dictionary. It was like this: when she was certain that no one was watching, she took this dictionary from her father's desk and, thrilled at the forbidden pleasure (for her conscience told her this was bad), she let her hungry eyes feed. Under "Man" there is a two page anatomical diagram. You can see the skeleton, the muscles stripped bare; but a naked man, an athlete girded with a tight animal skin, with a full head of hair, is shown from the front and the rear, in the pose of a pugilist, which makes his abdomen, pectoral muscles, shoulder muscles, and thighs stand out.

Eliane never tired of looking at this picture, sometimes brushing the paper lightly with her lips.

She easily ignored the arrows and the words indicating and naming the different parts of this lovely body: occiput, medius, abdomen, epigastrium. She turned him into a living being, a character like Prince Charming; she made up adventures, novels, in which he was the hero. But then her imagination quickly ran dry; it was so much more agreeable just to look at him. She could have spent hours contemplating the naked man, but children are never left alone for long.

Besides, about a year ago Eliane stopped being Prince

Charming's love, and she exhausted all the knowledge in the Illustrated Dictionary. Now, taking infinite precautions without seeming to, trembling at the thought of her mother noticing her behavior, Eliane began to watch men.

It is an education. At first she found that they were all ugly and, moreover, insignificant, preoccupied with mundane things, enemies of dreams, as useless as shadows or dead people. Really, Prince Charming and the beautiful Greek wrestler didn't match up with anything in real life. But, little by little, one's vision adjusts itself, one's taste frees itself from schools of thought; beauty no longer needs to be shown in order to be seen; the artist breaks away from his masters, and the young lover learns to create for herself—from passers-by, from half-naked grape pickers, from a worker standing on a scaffold—chosen lovers, creatures of beauty, spirits that are powerful, refined and heroic, with the souls of poets and conquerors. The completely abstract worship of virile forms was no longer enough for Eliane; that was a purely intellectual adoration, in which the heart played too small a role.

What was the beautiful wrestler himself without a soul, without a life of feelings and thought? But Eliane began with a preference for watching laborers, those beautiful bare-chested lads who toil in the sun. This was still an admiration for naked flesh, bulging muscles, flat chests, narrow hips, hard arms. Besides, the fat burghers are truly hideous. In front they carry paunches dilated by lengthy excesses of food, their hair is falling out, their cheeks hang, their noses are turning red, and their eyes are clouding over. But they can't be like that at twenty. Eliane didn't take long to notice this. And then, we must content ourselves with whatever life has to offer, free from exaggeration. She came to discover a kind of more delicate beauty in a few students that she saw during short visits in the streets of the county seat.

And now there are thirty-year-old men everywhere; gentlemen with lovely beards, with self-confident yet gentle looks in their eyes.

Eliane is overjoyed to see them, to tread the same ground that they walk upon. But she doesn't succeed, poor dreamer, in interesting herself in what goes on in the course of everyday life. Mediocre destinies don't concern her in the least. She will demand of her future loves adventurous lives, brilliant actions, popularity, glory. And all this must exist somewhere, but not here, not in her surroundings. Anyway, isn't she like a prisoner? "Oh, if only I were twenty!" She thinks that's the age of freedom.

She is sure that there are wonderful beings in the world: their whole lives are poems; they win battles, organize widespread popular movements; they pass quickly from extreme poverty to the most fabulous wealth; they are beautiful, they are famous, and they scorn the petty things in life. Eliane was raised in the Reformed Church; she'll receive her communion next year, but the most well-defined part of her religious instruction is an in-depth knowledge of the Song of Songs, read and re-read from the huge family Bible. And since her father, who is a free thinker, has too often mocked what he calls the extravagances of the saints and martyrs in front of her, she feels nothing but disgust for humility and obedience. She scorns weakness and poverty, and is horrified by the sick. Because of this, the Wonderful Beings are all strong and triumphant. She communicates with them in the spiritual world; she is their little wife.

But each of these noble souls needs its own body. Eliane chooses the man who embodies her dream of the moment. She takes his features into her memory, carefully preserves the memory of his walk, and closes her eyes in order to recall him better. And it's just like it was with Prince Charming; but reality is finally lending some nourishment to this fantasy which, henceforth, no longers functions in a void.

Eliane is thinking about someone who really exists. Eliane has a Beloved, several Beloveds, and a host of lovers. One Beloved that's a little vague, one Ideal; but also other Beloveds, chosen from among the young people from her little town; their features are familiar to her. Some of them, in real life, even know her family and sometimes will make a few casual remarks to her. But while she pretends to learn her lessons and do her homework, she is living by their sides, she is accompanying them on thousands of adventures, military expeditions, and explorations. Sometimes her imaginary companion is one person, sometimes another.

She especially thinks of them—or one of them—in her bed, right before falling asleep. Each one gets his turn, each one gets his night according to Eliane's mood.

Sometimes she stays faithful to one of her Beloveds every night for a whole week.

He is lying next to her, they kiss, she caresses him

with burning hands, he returns her caresses. She falls asleep in his arms.... And there's a crowd of all the charming and quickly-erased memories she recalled for one night: officers, gypsies selling baskets, men of the world, a young sailor.

Eliane believes in the transmission of thoughts. She doesn't want to think that all this love, all these longings, will disappear without ever touching the souls they address so passionately. Aren't they also dreaming of her on those nights? Don't the ones that she chooses at least experience some inexplicable sensation of pleasure? If only she could be sure; she would ask nothing more. And yet, what if, one day, one of her Beloveds deigned to notice her, to come to her, to speak to her secretly? For him, no matter who he was, even if he was the least desired of all of them, but a real love that she could clasp in her arms—ah! How quickly she would abandon all those sterile dreams that she wears herself out with....

At the end of her last summer vacation the farmhouse was full of grape-pickers. She noticed one of them; his pants hitched up to his knees, his shirtsleeves rolled up to his shoulders, his shirt thrown open—revealing an admirable golden chest—and the refined head of a young man, with big brown eyes full of tender glances. Eliane asked him for a bunch of grapes; she had never been so bold before.

And all night in her stifling bedroom, panting, sweating, she wishes that he, the handsome grape-picker, would come.

She told herself that if she wished hard enough, if she concentrated with all the force of her will, he would hear her. At one moment it seemed as if the latch on the door creaked. She sat up in her bed, gasping: she was so certain that she could make him come.

Finally she stopped hoping, and suddenly she began to sob with rage. The next day when she awoke she could feel the dried tears on her slightly pale cheeks. She kissed her reflection in the mirror for a long time. She felt very sorry for herself.

Yes, if she could meet her Beloved!.... And yet, men don't lack boldness. To spend an hour with the object of their love they scale balconies, force doors, and risk their lives. Alas! Eliane is still only a little girl, with hair down her back and short skirts, and men do not pay homage to well-behaved little girls who are always accompanied by their mothers or their maids. Oh, beautiful, soft eyes of Eliane, don't they understand the language you speak?

Yes, if she could meet her Beloved.... Yet perhaps she'd be the one to run from him, unwilling to leave her dreams....

"Eliane!" calls her mother, with her strong Minervois accent. Eliane trembles. "Mother?"

"Are you still in the clouds? Why are you still sitting there staring into space like a ninny? Go take your little brother for a walk in the shade, to the end of the lawn, and be careful, do be careful...."

Eliane obeys: she gets up, takes her brother by the hand, and guides him toward the see-saw under the nettle trees. How far her thoughts were from her mother and her little brother, and from the pretty park!.... If only she could meet her Beloved....

But, truly, this would only be the beginning of her

happiness, the vacation to end all vacations. She wouldn't love him; or rather, while loving him, she would keep her independence; she would only give half of herself. Whereas he would give himself without reservation. She looks forward to his arrival, and the revelation that he would bring her, the way one looks forward to reading a book, or taking a trip to a distant country. But this would be so much more important than a book or a trip!

And then there's this: to learn by experience exactly what role one can play in the existence of these unknown beings; to try to control them, to guess their goals and their reasons for living.

She would not say to him, as to Prince Charming, "I am your humble slave." Or maybe, after all, she would say it, but she would be lying.

The "mistress"—to be someone's mistress.

In Minervois the big wine merchants often have two households. They talk about these things in front of Eliane practically every day. She understands very well that the wives are pitied for being obliged to share, and that the mistresses are heaped with scorn. "Those girls don't die, they croak," says her mother. On the other hand, it's obvious that the world blackens with its scorn and pursues with its hatred everything that is noble and pure, anything that transcends its weighty common sense, its natural baseness. Eliane has figured this out, and she shudders with rage and with pride when her mother says, "Why can't you behave like everyone else?" or when she cries out, in front of some ladies that are visiting, "Oh, Lord, how this daughter worries me, she is so withdrawn, she will never be like everyone else." And she secretly feels sorry for the mistresses and admires them; she would like to get to know them; she feels they are sisters who would understand her. These petty intrigues of the jovial and brutal merchants interest her as much as the great passions of George Sand, of whom she has secretly read a few incomplete volumes that she found in the bottom of a drawer in her bedroom.

Eliane picks up her little brother and kisses him gently. Then she hums. She wonders: "Can I really please someone?" Then she dreams again of the lovely songs about blondes, the songs that she doesn't dare sing in front of her mother, and that she never listens to without blushing a little: "My Lovely Blonde Angel" and "Blonde Queen, Far from the World." That's what you call songs with feeling!

Eliane breathes deeply; she climbs the see-saw in one huge step and immediately regrets having given in to this bit of childishness, because two young men have just stepped into the park.

Walking slowly, they follow the pathway that circles the lawn. Eliane judges them in one glance; they belong to the crowd of those who are indifferent to her, and of whom she will remember nothing; two young men, no more, no less.

She thinks of a student whom she passed a little while ago in Theatre Street. His red striped beret barely covered his unruly mass of black hair and revealed a large, clear forehead. In her memory she reviews all his features, his nonchalant strides. Did he even see her? Why is she afraid to look people in the eye? What difference does it make if they can read her thoughts? It's just as well, really: it would be like the beginning of an intrigue, a secret between her and a few strangers. But if only she dared...talk to someone. This would also be a way to stop being the stupid butt of her mother's jokes: she wouldn't stop being obedient and resigned, but in the midst of these great deafening bubblings of revolt she would dream of...well, of him! And this thought would calm and avenge her.

The two young men just passed by, close to Eliane. She looked each one of them in the eye, for no reason, just to practice. But her glance met that of the young man on the left, closest to the lawn; he is small, dark. She let herself be taken by surprise; and he fixed his glance upon hers for a long moment as he continued his conversation.

Eliane is still thinking about her mother, not with anger but with despair; she puts up with her the way one would put up with prison, or a long illness. "That woman" makes Eliane use her old boots under the pretext that they both wear the same size; Eliane tells herself that she'd rather go barefoot. *They* pass by again; it's their second time around. And again the young brown-haired man meets Eliane's glance. And then, as she becomes bolder, they look at each other for a few seconds. He admires her fresh cheeks and her beautiful eyes with their dark rings; and her glances, astonished, happy, sometimes embarrassed, sometimes offended, retreat and emerge, refuse and yield. These glances practically tremble.

The other young man sees nothing of these goings-on. He is giving drawn-out explanations to his friend.

"You see, Lucien...." Eliane thinks dreamily: "His name is Lucien. Your name is like wafting perfume." And she walks toward Lucien, under the pretext of extending the child's walk. But now her mother, who interrupts her knitting, lifts her head just as Lucien passes close to Eliane, and shouts:

"Eliane! Now, don't go so far!" Eliane stops dead in her tracks. "He heard, now he knows my name." And, without knowing exactly why, that makes her happy.

And Lucien, with his friend, continues to circle the lawn and, every time he meets Eliane, a new exchange of looks brings them closer together. What can he be thinking of her? It looks as if he is not displeased by her village dress, what he can see of the simple scallop-work on her calico skirt, the ribbed stockings, and her mother's worn-out boots. Oh, Lucien, you aren't handsome, but right now you are the most beloved, because you are the first one to look at her like this!

Now she's returned to her mother's side. They stand a few steps from each other while the child, with tiny, clumsy steps, walks from one to the other, his dizziness showing in his eyes. Eliane bends over him, her long hair hanging in her face. She cries, "Ah, how funny he is, the dear child, oh!" Lucien passes, he is next to her. Then, suddenly, as if still speaking to the child, but for Lucien alone, she adds the words from the books, the incommensurable words, "I love you." What a strangled voice, a voice suffocated with fear, made deep and deaf by the emotion of such a confession, her first declaration of love. The order of nature remains unchanged. A sunbeam creates a lovely arc of colors in the humid spray of the fountain. How clear the air is! There is nothing to set off this major event in Eliane's life. But in her ears is the noise of her own voice, the sound of the terrible words that she has just uttered, like the rumble of a thunderclap.

Finally she recovers her composure. Her mother was taken in by her ruse, or maybe she didn't even hear. But Lucien understood; and when he passes again, his eyes gravely tell her so. The joy inside her is like a torrent. Finally! Someone knows the wonderful secret.

And she gets braver. The two friends will soon be next to her. She walks in front of them, in spite of her mother, who shouts to her that she shouldn't tire out the child, that she should come back and sit beside her. Eliane doesn't hear anything. She steps between the lawn and Lucien, and, because of the lack of space, he brushes against her involuntarily. She had planned this. Lucien bows, murmurs, "Excuse me, mademoiselle." Eliane decides to listen to her mother.

And when she is comfortably sitting in the chair with her brother on her lap, she looks up to see Lucien and his friend leaving the park. She thinks, "Now there is a secret between Lucien and me; I love, and I am loved." Again, one mustn't ask too much of life.

The train they have been waiting for, the train home, will soon be announced at the station. Eliane, calmed, smiles sadly: "Adieu, Lucien." The street corner has just hidden him from her view.

Is there anything more important than the memory of a childhood declaration, and the reflection in it of a hundred frank and trembling blue-eyed glances?

Valéry Larbaud

Valéry Larbaud was born in Vichy, France in 1881. As a child Larbaud attended school in South America, and his literary tastes, essays, poems, and novels, bear the influences of his cosmopolitan upbringing and later travels. He describes his South American background, in part, in his early novella *Fermina Marquez* (1911), and in his most famous work, *Journal d'A. O. Barnabooth* (1913), whose protagonist is a wealthy and bored South American multi-millionaire. *Enfantines* (1918) and *Amants, heureux amants* (1924) further reveal his attention to style and international literary influences.

Larbaud was also a noted translator, critic and linguist, bringing into French several American and English writers such as Walt Whitman, James Joyce, and Joseph Conrad.

Larbaud received the *Grand Prix National des Lettres* in 1952. He died in 1957.

SUN & MOON CLASSICS

The Sun & Moon Classics is a publicly supported, nonprofit program to publish new editions, translations, or republications of outstanding world literature of the late nineteenth and twentieth centuries. Through its publication of living authors as well as great masters of the century, the series attempts to redefine what usually is meant by the idea of a "classic" by dehistoricizing the concept and embracing a new, ever changing literary canon.

Organized by the Contemporary Arts Educational Project, Inc., a nonprofit corporation, and published by its program, Sun & Moon Press, the series is made possible, in part, by grants and individual contributions.

This book was made possible, in part, through matching grants from the National Endowment for the Arts and from the California Arts Council, through an organizational grant from the Andrew W. Mellon Foundation, through a grant for advertising and promotion from the Lila Wallace/Reader's Digest Fund, and through contributions from the following individuals:

Charles Altieri (Seattle, Washington)
John Arden (Galway, Ireland)
Jesse Huntley Ausubel (New York, New York)
Dennis Barone (West Hartford, Connecticut)
Jonathan Baumbach (Brooklyn, New York)
Guy Bennett (Los Angeles, California)
Bill Berkson (Bolinas, California)
Steve Benson (Berkeley, California)
Charles Bernstein and Susan Bee (New York, New York)
Sherry Bernstein (New York, New York)
Dorothy Bilik (Silver Spring, Maryland)
Bill Corbett (Boston, Massachusetts)
Fielding Dawson (New York, New York)
Robert Crosson (Los Angeles, California)
Tina Darragh and P. Inman (Greenbelt, Maryland)
David Detrich (Los Angeles, California)
Christopher Dewdney (Toronto, Canada)
Philip Dunne (Malibu, California)
George Economou (Norman, Oklahoma)
Elaine Equi and Jerome Sala (New York, New York)
Lawrence Ferlinghetti (San Francisco, California)
Richard Foreman (New York, New York)
Howard N. Fox (Los Angeles, California)
Jerry Fox (Aventura, Florida)

In Memoriam: Rose Fox
Melvyn Freilicher (San Diego, California)
Miro Gavran (Zagreb, Croatia)
Peter Glassgold (Brooklyn, New York)
Barbara Guest (New York, New York)
Perla and Amiram V. Karney (Bel Air, California)
Fred Haines (Los Angeles, California)
Fanny Howe (La Jolla, California)
Harold Jaffe (San Diego, California)
Ira S. Jaffe (Albuquerque, New Mexico)
Alex Katz (New York, New York)
Tom LaFarge (New York, New York)
Mary Jane Lafferty (Los Angeles, California)
Michael Lally (Santa Monica, California)
Norman Lavers (Jonesboro, Arkansas)
Jerome Lawrence (Malibu, California)
Stacey Levine (Seattle, Washington)
Herbert Lust (Greenwich, Connecticut)
Norman MacAffee (New York, New York)
Rosemary Macchiavelli (Washington, DC)
Beatrice Manley (Los Angeles, California)
Martin Nakell (Los Angeles, California)
Toby Olson (Philadelphia, Pennsylvania)
Maggie O'Sullivan (Hebden Bridge, England)
Rochelle Owens (Norman, Oklahoma)
Marjorie and Joseph Perloff (Pacific Palisades, California)
Dennis Phillips (Los Angeles, California)
David Reed (New York, New York)
Ishmael Reed (Oakland, California)
Janet Rodney (Santa Fe, New Mexico)
Joe Ross (Washington, DC)
Dr. Marvin and Ruth Sackner (Miami Beach, Florida)
Floyd Salas (Berkeley, California)
Tom Savage (New York, New York)
Leslie Scalapino (Oakland, California)
James Sherry (New York, New York)
Aaron Shurin (San Francisco, California)
Charles Simic (Strafford, New Hampshire)
Gilbert Sorrentino (Stanford, California)
Catharine R. Stimpson (Staten Island, New York)
John Taggart (Newburg, Pennsylvania)
Nathaniel Tarn (Tesuque, New Mexico)

If you would like to be a contributor to this series, please send your tax-deductible contribution to The Contemporary Arts Educational Project, Inc., a non-profit corporation, 6026 Wilshire Boulevard, Los Angeles, California 90036.

Books in the Sun & Moon Classics

1 Gertrude Stein *Mrs. Reynolds*
2 Djuna Barnes *Smoke and Other Early Stories*
3 Stijn Streuvels *The Flaxfield**
4 Marianne Hauser *Prince Ishmael*
5 Djuna Barnes *New York*
6 Arthur Schnitzler *Dream Story*
7 Susan Howe *The Europe of Trusts*
8 Gertrude Stein *Tender Buttons*
9 Arkadii Dragomoschenko *Description**
10 David Antin *Selected Poems: 1963-1973**
11 Lyn Hejinian *My Life***
12 F. T. Marinetti *Let's Murder the Moonshine: Selected Writings*
13 Heimito von Doderer *The Demons*
14 Charles Bernstein *Rough Trades**
15 Fanny Howe *The Deep North**
16 Tarjei Vesaas *The Ice Palace*
17 Jackson Mac Low *Pieces O' Six**
18 Steve Katz *43 Fictions**
19 Valery Larbaud *Childish Things**
20 Wendy Walker *The Secret Service**
21 Lyn Hejinian *The Cell**
22 Len Jenkin *Dark Ride and Other Plays**
23 Tom Raworth *Eternal Sections**

24 Ray DiPalma *Numbers and Tempers: Selected Poems**
25 Italo Svevo *As a Man Grows Older*
26 André Breton *Earthlight**
27 Fanny Howe *Saving History**
28 F. T. Marinetti *The Untameables*
29 Arkadii Dragomoschenko *Xenia**
30 Barbara Guest *Defensive Rapture**
31 Carl Van Vechten *Parties*
32 David Bromige *The Harbormaster of Hong Kong**
33 Keith Waldrop *Light While There is Light: An American History**
34 Clark Coolidge *The Rova Improvisations**
35 Dominique Fourcade *Xbo**
36 Marianne Hauser *Me & My Mom**
37 Arthur Schnitzler *Lieutenant Gustl*
38 Wilhelm Jensen/Sigmund Freud *Gradiva/Delusion and Dream in Gradiva*
39 Clark Coolidge *Own Face*
40 Susana Thénon *distancias/distances**
41 José Emilio Pacheco *A Distant Death**
42 Lyn Hejinian *The Cold of Poetry***
43 Jens Bjørneboe *The Bird Lovers**
44 Gertrude Stein *Stanzas in Meditation*
45 Jerome Rothenberg *Gematria**
46 Leslie Scalapino *Defoe**
47 Douglas Messerli, ed. *From the Other Side of the Century: A New American Poetry 1960–1990**
48 Charles Bernstein *Dark City**
49 Charles Bernstein *Content's Dream: Essays 1975–1984*

*First American publication
**Revised edition

DATE DUE

FEB. 16 1995			
3/24/99	IL 900	1031	PPN